T0063348

# ONCE UPON A HIGH-RISE

J. Allan Woodard

**ONCE UPON A HIGH-RISE**



*iUniverse books may be ordered through booksellers or by contacting:*

*iUniverse LLC*
*1663 Liberty Drive*
*Bloomington, IN 47403*
*www.iuniverse.com*
*1-800-Authors (1-800-288-4677)*



*ISBN: 978-1-4917-4131-3 (sc)*
*ISBN: 978-1-4917-4132-0 (e)*

*Printed in the United States of America.*

*iUniverse rev. date: 09/02/2014*

# Chapter One

The July afternoon sun beat down unmercifully on Mark Winslow's head. Beads of sweat percolated from his scalp, racing through his prematurely grey hair, like ants to a picnic, eager to be the first to drip down his face and neck. He trudged along the edge of the highway muttering to himself while forcing one foot in front of the other.

*You've got to take a break from this case, Mark. You're a walking nervous breakdown looking for a place to happen, Mark. I can see them now, throwing darts at a map after they cut Hawaii, Bermuda and the Caribbean out. One of the darts lands on Atlanta muggy Georgia, and voila, that's where we'll send him... in the middle of July. Oh, he'll love it. Well, one more night of this crap and I'll resign and haul my ass back to the Rocky Mountains in Montana, where the summers are seventy degrees, both days of it...and we hope it falls on a weekend.* He laughed. He didn't care. No one could hear him.

Thankful that he left his sport coat in the rental that now sat umpteen miles back, he loosened his tie, unbuttoned the top three buttons of his sweat-soaked white Oxford shirt and rubbed the back of his neck. *I'll call and let them know where they can find their damn car, but I bet I'll never see that coat again.*

Wiping his face with his Dolcé & Gabbana silk necktie, a Christmas gift from his rich uncle, now hanging loosely around his neck, he thought, *Suck it up, Sport, you could be back in New York still searching for the bastards who raped and tortured those four young women.* Visions of the gruesome crime scenes mocked him yet again. Mark's heart rate soared and his insides twisted. He could almost smell the rancid stench of what they had found at each grisly scene. He couldn't get the vision of one of the victims out of his thoughts or dreams; no, they were nightmares. Bile rose up in his throat when he remembered her mutilated body, the cigarette burns on her breasts, and long surgical steel needles jammed through her cheeks and lips so she couldn't scream or beg for mercy. The look on her face of agonizing pain and fear, frozen there by death, haunted him day and night.

*Those vicious, bloodthirsty bastards were clever, leaving no clues, but every dog has his day and I'll get them yet. When I do I'll castrate...* Mark shook his head. *Maybe the Bureau Chief was right, I did need to get away from it.*

A large overhead road sign momentarily blocked the upper half of his body from the sun, bringing him back to the present. Downtown Atlanta — Four Miles. He looked back, trying to measure how far he'd walked, using the distance between himself and the rental. It was only a speck, almost indistinguishable as a car behind the shimmering heat mirages rising off the pavement. *How the hell do people live in this heat and humidity? The soles of my feet are frying in my shoes. When I get back to the hotel, if I get back there, I'm going to turn the air conditioner up to high, fill the tub with cold water and sit in it... Hell, I might even add a bucket of ice to it.* He grinned at the mental image.

Mark turned to walk backwards, extending the right arm he'd be willing to give away for a sip of water. *Maybe I should have stayed with the car. Well, it's too late to start second guessing myself. There's not a cloud in the sky or a house nearby to use a phone. And I'm the idiot who left my cell phone in the hotel room.*

The grey strip of road stretched for miles, bordered by sun scorched dried-up weeds that looked like overcooked bacon. Off in the distance above the trees, the tops of the buildings in downtown Atlanta were visible, so close. *Yeah, for a helicopter,* he mused.

Traffic raced past him — he felt like he was standing in front of a blast furnace with the door opening and closing.

Hoping someone would give him a ride, he pulled the leather badge wallet out of his back pocket, opened it and turned to walk backwards while displaying the badge. Checking behind him to be sure he wasn't about to back into a post or step in a hole, he turned and saw an emerald green Corvette Stingray cut across traffic and roar to a stop thirty feet ahead of him. He started to run toward the car. *Great, a young hot-shot, but at least it's a ride.* Mark jumped out of the way as the Corvette backed towards him. When it stopped he bent down and opened the door. "Thanks for stopping..." Surprised to see a stunning brunette behind the wheel, he quickly took in her classic white linen pant suit, beige silk blouse and a crazy looking necklace with matching earrings of walnut sized balls that looked like wood. A bit surprised, Mark started to laugh, "I... I'm..."

"Yes, I know," the woman smiled, "you expected to see a guy driving this thing. Get in, you're wasting all my air conditioning."

"Actually, I saw the New York plates and thought you might be someone I know." He hesitated, wondering how his six-five frame would fit. As soon as he was in, he found it quite roomy and settled himself in the comfortable black leather bucket seat, then pulled the door closed. "Thanks for stopping..."

She turned to look at him, "I wouldn't have if I didn't see that gold badge." Her eyes were the color of blue arctic ice, but her smile melted the chill. *I think I've seen him somewhere before.*

"Do you live in Atlanta? If it's not too far, I can give you a ride home."

"No, I'm from..."

"Oh," she interrupted, "I saw the Georgia license plates on the car back there and thought... Anyway, where are you staying?"

"At the Hilton Atlanta on Courtland Street. The car's a rental. I decided to do a little sightseeing — not one of my better ideas. I'm attending the American Bar Association's criminal defense section conference. This is the third and last day. Just have to sit through a couple of presentations tonight and listen to some woman give one of those boring after dinner speeches. Then I fly back to New York in the morning." Mark held up his badge to give her a closer look, then attempted to put it in his back pocket. His hand was pinned behind him as she stomped on the accelerator and moved out into traffic, cut across three lanes, shifting four times before settling in the left lane at what Mark estimated to be ninety miles an hour.

"How many gears does this thing have?"

"Seven. Why do you ask?"

"Just curious."

"We're attending the same convention. I'm the woman giving the boring after dinner speech tonight."

*Open mouth, insert foot!* "Oh, I thought you were here to teach Jeff Gordon how to drive his race car."

"You're very funny. I hope you don't mind if I turn the air conditioning up to full blast. Maybe you'll catch pneumonia and won't have to listen to my boring speech."

*Maybe I don't need the air conditioner with that bone-chilling look you just gave me.* "I hope your speech isn't about safe driving."

She shot him a look. "You could find yourself walking again if you keep going with those witty comments."

"Okay, I give up," Mark laughed. "Are you here with anyone?"

"No, I'm on my own."

"Law enforcement?"

"Defense attorney. Are you here with your wife?" she asked, down shifting to use the engine to brake the car, swearing under her breath when an idiot cut in front of her without warning.

Mark braced himself with his feet firmly on the floor. "No, I'm a widower."

"Oh... I'm sorry for your loss," she replied, sincerely.

Mark changed the subject, not wanting to talk about his wife's accident and wondered if he'd ever be able to talk about it without the embarrassing tears welling in his eyes. "I'm Mark Winslow; Captain

Winslow, CDS, with the New York City Police Department."

"What's the CDS stand for?"

"Commander Detective Squad."

"My name is Kristen Miller, I'm a criminal attorney with Gillis, Davies and Bernstein. The partners flew in with their wives today; I'm meeting them at the hotel. Attorney Davies is being inducted into the American Bar Association's criminal defense hall of fame tonight."

Mark recognized the name of the Manhattan law firm. He remembered where he had met her — and hoped *she* wouldn't recall, at least until he was within walking distance of the hotel. "Yesterday, I was asked to preside over one of the seminars the attorneys attend to get credits to comply with New York's annual mandatory legal education requirements. When I say I presided, all I did was hand out papers and collect pencils," he laughed.

"Did I just detect a cowboy drawl?"

Mark smiled and did his best John Wayne, "Sure did, Ma'am. Raised on a ranch in the Rocky Mountains of Montana."

*They grow them tall in those mountains.* "Are you on temporary assignment in New York?"

"No, I moved there with my daughter after my wife died."

"How old is your daughter?"

"Pamela is six years old."

"Oh, she's very young. Is she here with you?"

"No, she's with her maternal grandparents in Connecticut. She enjoys staying there, they spoil her," he said, grinning.

"Does she live with them?"

"No, just stays with them when I'm away or working long hours."

"It must be handy having your in-laws nearby, considering your line of work and the hours you must have to put in."

"Exactly. Tell me something, if the partners flew in, why did you drive all this way?"

"They fly first class. I don't. And I wanted to stop on the way to visit a couple of friends. I keep thinking I've seen you before."

"I was hoping you wouldn't remember."

"Oh," she smiled, "did you date someone I know?"

"I doubt that. Dating isn't on my list of hobbies."

"Well, I'll think of it."

"Perhaps you saw me at the hotel yesterday," he said, hoping to throw her off the hole she was digging to put him in, at least until he was within walking distance of the hotel.

"I wasn't here yesterday. No, it was definitely in New York." Tapping her chin with a manicured finger, "For some reason I think it may have been in court. Give me a second, it will come to me." Without warning she careened across three lanes and aimed for the exit, down shifting through the gears and cut in front of a tractor-trailer that was just entering the exit ramp.

Mark stomped his size fourteens to the floorboard. "Jesus Christ, are you trying to get us killed?"

"Oh. My. God! I know where I met you!"

"Damn." *Well, at least I'm off the highway, because I'm going to be walking.*

"State of New York versus Barrett. You!" she shrieked. "I was Barrett's defense attorney. Actually, I was a public defender at the time. You beat the hell out of me while I was cross-examining you. My client got life without parole because of you."

"No, he got life, because he was guilty. He was also a psychopathic liar."

Kristen pounded out her frustration on the steering wheel. "You buried me in that court room."

"I'd say I'm sorry, but I'm not. He was guilty."

She fixed her eyes on the road. "Okay, I'll admit you were right. Barrett made a comment immediately after the trial about something that only the murderer would have known and I knew then that the jury had made the right decision. He wants to file an appeal. I keep telling him we don't have any grounds for one. I positively know he's guilty, by his own stupidity and arrogance, and I don't want him back out on the streets." Kristen smiled, "Cowboy, you had him nailed."

***

Kristen down shifted several times and purred to a stop at the valet parking area in front of the Hilton. The attendant hurried to open her door as she popped the trunk to give the bellhop access to her luggage.

Mark, literally, hauled himself up and out of the car then turned and watched Kristen gracefully glide out in one fluid motion. He smiled, wondering how the hell she made it look so easy.

Kristen removed the extra ignition key from the key ring and handed the key to the attendant. "This car is equipped with an electronic valet parking device, so park it like you own it or the alarm will go off on my key ring and your ass will be grass and I'll be the lawnmower."

"Yes, Ma'am." He handed her the claim ticket. She slipped him a generous tip, then turned toward the door and saw Mark waiting for her. "I'm sorry, you didn't have to wait for me." *But I'm glad you did. There's just something about this guy. Not just his good looks.*

"No problem, unless you'd rather not be seen with me. I must look like a drowned rat."

Kristen laughed and hooked her arm through his as they walked into the crowded lobby.

"I've never heard of an electronic valet parking device, did it come with the car or was it an after market install?"

"As far as I know there's no such thing. I just say that so they don't mess with the car."

Mark burst out laughing, drawing a few quizzical looks. "Very clever. Hey, if you have time before your speech tonight, I'd like to take you to dinner to thank you for rescuing me."

"Oh, that would have been lovely, Mark, but I'm at the same table with the partners and their wives. And I think dinner will be served before any of the speeches. At least that's what I understood."

He wasn't sure if this was a brush off. "Yeah, you're right. I think it's roasted chicken tonight. I didn't know if you'd be at the banquet or just the presentation and speeches."

"You're very thoughtful. Perhaps we could meet afterward for drinks."

"Great! That's if I'm still awake when you get done with your boring part of the evening."

Kristen gently pinched his arm. "This is the part where you're supposed to be nice to me."

The partners of the law firm and their wives were checking in at the counter. Dan Davies tapped John Gillis on the shoulder, "Who's that tall guy with Kristen?"

"Holy crap, that's Mark Winslow, NYPD."

Mrs Gillis whispered, "I thought she hated him."

"Perhaps she doesn't recognize him," John Gillis replied.

Harvey Bernstein laughed, "It doesn't look like hate to me. We'll ask her later at the table."

The three wives looked at each other with glints in their eyes, all but rubbing their hands together, fresh gossip was their forte.

Mark walked Kristen to the end of the check-in queue, "After you leave the podium tonight I'll watch to see where you're sitting. When this shindig is over I'll come by the table and we'll go for that drink."

"Sounds like a plan. And I'll be watching you while I'm boring everyone, so try to stay awake."

"I'll try," he laughed, suddenly feeling the urge to kiss her. *Where the hell did that come from?* "I'll see you later. If you need to change the plan I'm in room six-two-zero."

Kristen watched him walk away and waited to see if he'd turn and look at her. If he didn't, she'd know this wasn't going anywhere.

Mark squeezed into the packed elevator, turned and winked at Kristen as the doors closed.

*What the hell am I thinking. Jessica hasn't been gone that long. And I don't have time for this right now. Drinks after and that's it. Definitely it. I do like her, she doesn't mince words. Has a sense of humor. Definitely a ten on the gorgeous meter. And it's been six years since... If this was the other way around would I have expected Jessica to be alone and lonely the rest of her life? Hell no. I'd be dead. I'd want her to move on, find someone she could be happy with, raise our children in a loving relationship.* Deep in thought, he got off on the wrong floor. Mark ran his fingers through his hair while he waited for the next elevator. *I'm going to need therapy.*

***

While unpacking and making sure there were no wrinkles in the mint green outfit she planned to wear later, Kristen laid it out neatly on the second queen bed and thought about calling her friend and associate, Carol. Instead, she decided to arrange the outfit to see how it would look altogether. She placed the necklace of magnesite turquoise nuggets at the collar of the suit jacket and the matching earrings just above that. Then slipped the left wrist of the suit into the matching magnesite bracelet and placed the double finger ring with the large ceramic turquoise flower petals at the right sleeve. The shoes, dyed to match the suit, were on the floor in front of what looked like a person on the bed, but without the body.

She shook her head and thought, *Maybe I do have ADD... or is it ADHD?* Deciding she didn't have either one, she went into the bathroom and made a project of lining up her toiletries — comb, hair brush, the tube containing her tooth brush, tooth paste, make-up and perfume — then unwrapped the bar of Kiehl's L'Occitane soap she brought with her, and placed it in the shower stall soap tray. Planning to wear her hair down, she didn't bother to plug in the blow dryer, but placed it on the counter just in case her hair got wet in the shower. Upset that she didn't pack her shower cap, she searched the complimentary amenities tray, spotted the tiny box marked SHOWER CAP and struggled to open the box. *Do they really want me to use this thing or don't they? If I break a fingernail...*

Thinking to take a fifteen minute power nap after her quick shower, she set the alarm clock on the bedside table, placed her cell phone beside it and snuggled between the cool sheets. She was just dozing off when the cell phone rang and announced — CAROL BENNETT.

*There goes the nap*, she thought as she reached for the phone. "Hi Carol, I was just thinking of calling you. Is everything okay at the office?"

"All is well. I'm just making sure you arrived safely."

"I got here about an hour ago."

"Anything exciting happen on the way?"

"Not that I can think of."

"Oh really? That's not what I heard."

Kristen laughed. "I should have known when I saw the three busybodies in the lobby."

"Actually, it was John Gillis who called, not one of the wives. He said you had a hitchhiker named Mark Winslow, *Captain* Mark Winslow."

"Yes, I did. John cornered me while I was checking in. He thought Mark and I had made the trip together. Actually, Mark's rental broke down just outside Atlanta, so I stopped to give him a ride. I didn't realize who he was until we were halfway to the hotel."

"And..?"

"And what? I drove him to the hotel. He asked if he could buy me a drink later, sort of a thank you for, as he put it, rescuing him."

"I thought you hated him?"

"Well, I do, I mean I did."

"But not anymore?" Carol goaded.

"He's very nice once you get to know him. Did you know he's a widower?"

"Yes. I think every eligible woman in Manhattan knows that. But from what I understand, he doesn't date. Not at all. John said he overheard Mark giving you his room number. What's up with that?"

"Jeez, Carol, that was only in case I changed my mind about having a drink with him later. Christ, now I dread sitting at the same table with all of them."

"If they get too nosey just look upset or nervous and Dan will shut them up. He's good at that."

"Carol, I really like Mark. What else do you know about him?"

"Well, he's been decorated several times in the line of duty. That was in the news, but I don't remember why. He has a daughter. I think she's five or six years old."

"Yes, he mentioned her. She's six."

"His wife and son were killed in an auto accident about four or five years... Now that I think about it, it may have been six years ago. They lived in Montana, then. I think his wife was on the way back home... If I recall, she was visiting someone on the east coast. Anyway, a drunk driver crossed the median and smashed into her head-on."

"No wonder he was nervous about the way I drive."

"Well, my only suggestion to that would be..." Carol hesitated.

"Yes, what?"

"If you go anywhere together, let him drive."

"You witch," Kristen laughed, "I thought you had some great insight into a budding romance."

Carol thought, *No, but I'm thrilled to see one about to start.* "As a matter of fact, you know more about him than you realize. I was assigned a case about six months ago that he was involved with. You might remember it, that teenager who tried to hold up a liquor store. The old guy behind the counter had a heart attack in the middle of the robbery. The kid, instead of taking the money and running, stopped and called for an ambulance."

"Yes, I remember that."

"And I'll never forget it." Carol went on with the story.

Kristen sighed, remembering his western drawl. "I thought *you* had that case dismissed."

"No, it wasn't me. I didn't even get to present one word of my fabulous case. I just stood there with my mouth hanging open, astonished that anyone on the NYPD would have that much compassion."

Unexpectedly, the alarm clock buzzed.

"What the hell is that?" Carol asked.

"It's thc alarm clock, someone must have set it and forgot to turn it off," Kristen cleverly invented, not wanting Carol to know she had interrupted the nap. "Oh my god, look at the time. Carol, I've got to get ready or I'll be late. I'm really glad you called."

"Just a little advice. Decide if you're over Richard. If you are, and Mark Studmuffin makes a serious pass, then please go for it. You're thirty-two years old. It's time for you to be happy."

***

Before Mark went down to dinner he called his folks at their ranch in Montana, for their usual Thursday evening chat. His mother had to take an angel food cake out of the oven so he ended up talking to his dad while she was trying to set the cake pan upside down on a bottle to cool. "They sent me to Atlanta for three days to get away from that case I'm working on."

"It's really that bad?"

"Yeah, Pop, it's that bad."

"Well, you know if you ever need to unload, I'm always here to listen."

"Thanks, Pop. I know that. You've always been there for me, through thick and thin. I thought about coming home instead of coming to this hot, clammy vacation spot, but I only have three days — it uses up two days flying to and from Montana, which would only leave me one day at home. I hope to take at least a week; hopefully, two weeks within the next nine or ten months."

"Well, son, that gives us something to look forward to. Tell me a little about what's happening there." His dad, always perceptive, knew that his son just needed to talk.

"It's the American Bar Association's Criminal Defense Section Conference. The attorneys can pick up continuing legal education credits. The seminar allows the attorneys to get credits to comply with New York's annual mandatory continuing legal education requirement. I was asked to sit in on one of the classes, you know, hand out papers and collect pencils. It gave me something to do. Tonight's the last night. There's a hall of fame induction ceremony and then back to the grind. There are a few reps from police departments, troopers, FBI and, of course, a lot of criminal attorneys."

"So the spouses have to find something to do to entertain themselves during the day?"

"Exactly. But they all go to the dinners at night and the induction ceremony tonight."

"Is it a big crowd?"

"I'd say so. A guesstimate would be thirty round tables that seat eight. The nice thing is there are place cards so each night we sit with a different group. It gives us a chance to exchange stories, have a few laughs, and refresh our repertoire of jokes. Oh, there's a couple of Texas Rangers, but they're too young to remember you."

"Everyone is too young to remember me," his dad chuckled.

"The first time the two Rangers, in Stetsons and cowboy boots, walked into the function room, there was a sudden hush, everyone was whispering, wondering why these two behemoths were here.

As you very well know, but most people don't, Rangers will hunt down a suspect to any state, they don't just work in Texas. Anyway, one Ranger took his hat off with great theatrics and said, 'Put your guns away, greenhorns, we're just here to rustle up some grub.' And the room exploded with laughter. I'm hoping they'll be at my table tonight."

"Oh, I wish I'd been there to see that."

"So do I, Pop, so do I."

"We never did wear official uniforms, the badge and hat were our identification. How about the other folks there, are they all decked out in their livery?"

"It's mostly attorneys in their expensive suits. There's a spattering of law enforcement. A few guys and gals wore their uniforms. Others squeezed into their Sunday best, you know, the stuff they grew out of years ago and only wear to funerals and weddings. And a few of us are in sport coats and slacks."

"Well, son, I won't hold you on the phone. Enjoy yourself."

"I will, Pop. And tell mom I said bye."

"Oh, before you hang up, your mother sends her love."

"Love to both of you. I'll call you next Thursday. Hopefully, I'll have a better idea of when Pamela and I can come for a visit."

"Do what you can, but don't worry about it. We'll talk to you next Thursday. Give our love to Pamela."

Mark was sure his dad hung up quickly before his mother could pester him for a definite date that she could write on her calendar, of when he'd be back to the ranch for a visit. She didn't like things 'wishy-washy'.

He clicked off his cell, looked in the mirror to be sure his necktie was straight and headed out the door. Mark was still smiling when the elevator doors opened.

***

The banquet was in full swing by the time he walked into the room. Attorney Kristen Miller was on the stage giving her speech. She looked gorgeous in a mint green suit with a long skirt and what looked like green rocks around her neck and dangling from her ears.

The waiters and waitresses were clearing the last few tables.

Mark made his way to a table where he saw an empty seat and checked the place card. It wasn't his name, but he sat anyway since he'd be facing the podium. The only woman at the table was seated next to him. He'd bet dollars to donuts she was FBI — plain black suit, nondescript earrings. They always had a certain look about them.

FBI leaned toward him and whispered, "You're late. You missed the meal."

Mark looked at her and smiled to acknowledge her reprimand and thought, *No shit, Sherlock. What gave you the clue, my stomach rumbling?*

A sergeant, looking sharp in his dress blues, sitting directly across the table, was waving his empty glass trying to get the attention of a server, any server.

FBI reached for the insulated coffee carafe and whispered loud enough for the sergeant to hear, "Stop waving that glass around, it's very rude."

Mark leaned a little closer to FBI, "Are you two married?"

"Hell no," she whispered, "I've never seen him before."

Mark chuckled to himself, *now I know why what's his name on the place card chose not to sit here,* and then reached for one of the decorated donuts.

FBI indicated toward the stage with her thumb and whispered, "Her idea. Cop food for dessert."

Mark poured himself a cup of coffee and nibbled at the donut. Suddenly there was a notable silence. *Uh-oh, she's finished talking and I haven't even pretended to listen.* He turned his head as nonchalantly as he could and saw a ring the size of a dinner plate on her right hand, then looked up at her face and realized she was smiling at him.

Kristen waited a few seconds until she held his attention. "Since the theme of this convention is about working with law enforcement and compassion in the penal system, I'd like to take a little detour here and tell you a brief story about true compassion. Just before I came downstairs this evening, I found out that six months ago an associate of mine, Carol Bennett, was assigned a case involving a teenager who tried to hold up a liquor store in Manhattan. The old man behind the counter had a heart attack in the middle of the robbery."

Kristen glanced at Mark and knew she now had his full attention. His eyebrows were almost touching each other. "The boy, instead of taking the money and running, stopped and called for an ambulance.

Carol, my associate, had stayed up night after night working up a case, as she said, that would impress F. Lee Bailey" — she waited for the laughter to subside — "to get the teen off with a light sentence. The boy's mother was sick and he was stealing to buy her medicine. The mother's brother found out about it and retained our firm. Now, both sides were in the judge's chambers and the captain involved in the case told the judge that given the mitigating circumstances, he recommended that the teenager be placed in his uncle's care for one year. The uncle had agreed to call the captain once a month, or sooner if need be, as to the boy's progress. But the story doesn't end there. When the year is up, the captain arranged for the young man to then spend the summer on his family's ranch in Montana."

When the applause finally died down, Kristen smiled and said, "Unfortunately, the caped crusader forgot to pack his cape this weekend, because this afternoon I found him trudging along the highway, after his rental car overheated, and I gave him a ride back to the hotel. As I said, I only found out moments before my presentation tonight that 'Clark Kent' is, in fact, Captain Mark Winslow." Kristen looked at Mark. "What?" She looked at the audience. "He's trying to tell me something." She laughed. "You would rather that I hadn't mentioned your name? Oh, he's shaking his fist at me." Kristen laughed. "Don't be angry with me, Carol's the one who said your name is Studmuffin." The room exploded in laughter. "Stand up, Mark. He's shaking his head no. Ladies and gentlemen, I give you the man of the hour, Captain Mark Winslow of the NYPD."

The applause was impressive.

Mark mouthed the words, You are in serious trouble. He finally, reluctantly stood up and owned the most embarrassing moment of his life.

Kristen gathered her materials off the podium and walked to where Mark was now sitting. She stood behind him, placed her hands on his shoulders and leaned to whisper in his ear, "There's an extra seat at our table for you. The partners asked if you would join us for a drink."

Her warm breath in his ear set his pulse racing. He stood up and exchanged the usual spurious pleasantries with everyone at the table. The sergeant smiled and raised his glass in a toast, "You lucky son of a bitch."

Mark acknowledged with a crisp nod then turned and followed Kristen to the attorneys' table.

The partners stood and shook Mark's hand. John Gillis handled the introductions and then ordered a round of drinks. They were careful not to ask too many personal questions, but were very curious about the ranch and what he did in Montana, before coming to New York.

Esther Bernstein, the nosiest of the three gossipmongers, with a few too many martinis under her belt, was tapping her temple, obviously mulling something around in her head.

"Winslow, Winslow, was that a family member of yours who was killed in that head-on collision about four years ago?"

Mark's smile stiffened. "It was six years ago and yes, my wife and son were killed."

"We're very sorry to hear that." Dan Davies tried to change the subject. "Would anyone care for another drink?"

Ignoring Dan, she asked, "Were you driving?"

Paul Bernstein clamped onto his wife's arm and whispered, "Not now, Esther."

"Well, for Pete's sake, I'm only asking a simple question. I don't know why I can't just ask a..."

Mark set his glass gently on the table. "It's all right." He hesitated, not wanting to recall the tragic incident, knowing that talking about it would bring back the recurring nightmares that would wake him — always at the same point — his wife and son trapped in the car, their faces pressed against the windows, screaming his name for help as the car burst into flames, their hands clawing at the glass. Mark shuddered visibly and thought, *I'll get this over with and then I won't ever repeat it again.* "Mrs Bernstein, I was the sheriff in a small town in Montana, where my family's ranch is located. My wife, Jessica, was driving home with my son, Todd, after visiting with her parents in Connecticut. Her father was very ill at the time. On the way home, on Route 90 in South Dakota..."

Mrs Bernstein interrupted, "Did she fall asleep? I mean, that's an awful long way for a woman to drive alone. Shouldn't you have been..."

Mark could hear the underlying blame in her voice so he quickly interrupted. "A drunk driver crossed the median and hit my wife's car head-on. My son was two years old at the time. My wife was seven months pregnant with our second child."

Mrs Bernstein asked, "Were they wearing seatbelts? I mean, children are supposed to be in car seats. Was your son in a car seat?"

Mark had had enough. "Mrs Bernstein, you asked what happened. My son was killed instantly. My wife, Jessica, was badly burned, but was able to get the back door open and pulled my son *out of his car seat* and out of the flaming car. Many people stopped to help. My wife collapsed on the road where she delivered our second child, a baby girl, with the help of a woman who happened to be a nurse. The woman wrapped the baby in her own sweater. My wife was holding both children when she died. They told me she was smiling even though she was burned over seventy percent of her body."

Mrs Bernstein saw tears welling up in Mark's eyes, but couldn't let the question go unanswered. "The baby girl, what happened to the baby?"

Mark's eyes stung and his throat was tight with emotion, but he managed to smile, "She's alive and well. It was touch and go for about eight months, but my daughter, Pamela, is six years old now." Mark smiled, but the corners of his mouth pulsated involuntarily. "Pamela lives with me, but visits my in-laws quite often. She's with them now."

Kristen stared at her glass as she turned it methodically in her long, graceful fingers, her hands trembling, wondering how this man had survived such a horrific tragedy.

Mark stood up, looked at Kristen, then at the speechless group. "I have an early flight in the morning, so I'll say good night."

He was able to hold it together until he got into the empty elevator.

# Chapter Two

Kristen managed to get to her room without making a scene. Her body trembling and her hands shaking, it took several tries to unlock the door with the key card. Finally, she managed to get the door open, stepped in, closed the door and locked it with both locks. Then with an annoyed sigh, she unlocked and opened the door, placed the DO NOT DISTURB sign on the doorknob and closed and locked the door. She looked at the two queen size beds and knew her wobbly legs wouldn't carry her that far. Leaning back against the door, she slowly slid down until she was sitting on the floor with her knees bent in front of her face. And she sobbed, heart wrenching, gasping sobs. "I'll probably never see him again. Maybe I shouldn't have told that story." Her eye makeup ran down her face and onto her long mint green skirt. And she didn't care.

When she woke up, her legs were cramped, her arms were crossed over her knees and her head rested on her arms.

She looked at her watch. *I've been here for forty-five minutes. I can't stay like this all night. I'll take a shower and go to bed. I must have had more to drink than I thought.*

She turned on the bathroom light, twirled the shower knob to hot, stepped to the sink to put on the shower cap she had used earlier and was shocked when she saw the terrifying coal black face staring at her in the mirror. Finally, she realized it was her own face, the mascara had smeared around her eyes and rained down her cheeks. She leaned on the sink trying to regain her composure. When her heart finally stopped racing, she removed her clothes and tossed them on the floor. She would never, ever wear that outfit again.

Adjusting the water temperature, she stepped into the shower, scrubbed her face several times, then let the warm water refresh her. Finished, she quickly dried herself and snuggled into the thick white hotel robe that she found hanging on a hook on the back of the bathroom door. She walked to the bed that she had tried to nap in earlier and sat on the edge. Her anger grew, *Goddamn Mrs Bernstein didn't help any with her big mouth. She never knows when to shut that big gob of hers. She screwed up everything.*

Kristen walked to the window, closed the drapes, grabbed her suitcase and threw it on the bed. She knew she'd be sorry when she opened it in the morning, but she continued to toss everything in. *I don't care, I'm pissed, really, really pissed.*

She quickly pulled her sexy pink silk chemise and matching robe out of the suitcase before they got too wrinkled and let the white robe fall to the floor. *Even though I'm fuming, I don't have to look repulsive.* She gussied herself up in the silk chemise and robe, then sat on the bed and put her chin in her hand. *And I'm ticked at him, too. He didn't have to walk away from me.* "Just walks away from me." In a nasally voice she mimicked, "I have an early flight in the morning." *Yeah, well I have a long drive.* Kristen was working up a good head of steam.

She looked around the room, checked the bathroom to be sure she had everything she wanted — everything, except the mint green outfit that she swore she'd never wear again — zipped her suitcase, yanked up the handle, towed it out the door and headed for room six-two-zero.

***

Mark stepped out of the shower and was drying himself when he thought he heard a knock at the door. *Who the hell would knock at this time of night?*

There it was again.

*Yup, definitely a knock.* He grabbed a pair of light blue boxers, hopped to the door while trying to get them on and looked through the peephole, but couldn't see anything. Someone was definitely there, they knocked again.

Mark grabbed his SIG Sauer 9mm, racked a round into the chamber, flipped the safety off, held it down to his side and opened the door.

"Hi. You told me if the plans changed that you were in room six-two-zero. Plans have changed."

Mark started to laugh. "Did anyone see you parading around in that, that sexy get-up you're almost wearing?"

"I did get a couple of wolf whistles," she lied.

Mark put his bare foot against the door to hold it open, reached out, grabbed her arm and gently pulled her into the room. Quickly taking his foot out of the way, the door closed.

"Ohhh, a yummy doorman in blue boxers."

Mark flipped the safety on — he'd clear the chamber in the morning — then reached over and placed his SIG on the bureau.

"A gun? Why were you holding a gun?"

"Someone knocked on my door, I looked through the peephole and didn't see anyone. I wasn't opening the door without a weapon in my hand."

"I had my finger over the peephole."

"Why?"

"In case you saw me and wouldn't open the door. Oh, my suitcase is in the hall."

"Your suitcase? Are you leaving tonight dressed like that? Or is that your sleep in the car outfit?" he smirked.

"No, not dressed like this!"

"Well, why are you towing your suitcase around the hotel?"

"My plans changed."

He laughed, "You said that. Do you want to share those plans with me?"

"If you get my suitcase out of the hall before someone takes it, yes, I'll share those plans."

Mark gently moved Kristen out of the way and opened the door. He was in his boxers so he made sure no one was in the hall, stepped out, grabbed the suitcase and carried it in.

"The suitcase has wheels," she said.

"I'm aware of that, but I was in a hurry. I don't like being in the hallway in my underwear. Would you like to sit down?"

"Okay. But before I sit down, tomorrow I'm driving home, and I'm stopping in Virginia, to see my parents. Do you want to go with me?"

Without hesitation, Mark said, "Yes, if I do the driving."

"It's a deal."

Mark gestured to a chair.

Instead, Kristen sat on the edge of the bed.

*Okay, have it your way.* He sat in the chair, leaned forward with his arms resting on his knees and intertwined his fingers. He looked at Kristen. "Are you planning to spend the night in this room?"

"Gosh, that didn't take you too long to figure out."

"There's only one bed."

"It's big enough. King size, isn't it?"

"Kristen, I didn't bring anything with me."

"I thought all men carry a condom in their wallet just in case?"

"I don't. And if we get in that bed together it won't be to sleep."

"Oh good. I was afraid you weren't going to catch on this quickly. I'm on birth control to keep my cycle regular."

Mark stood up and pulled Kristen off the bed and into his arms. "I caught on, but didn't want to get my hopes up." He held her face in his hands and kissed her lips, her cheek, her ear, then slowly nibbled his way down her neck. He slipped his index fingers along the tops of her shoulders and under the pink pieces of fluff she was wearing — they quickly floated to her feet.

Kristen's hands moved smoothly down his back and under the elastic on his blue boxers and felt his firm butt. The boxers almost fell to the floor but got stuck up front. She maneuvered around that problem and they fell to the floor. Mark stepped out of them, reached behind her and pulled the spread and blanket down, then cradled her back and legs and lifted her to the center of the bed. "It's been a long time for me, so this might be quick."

"As long as it's slower the second time."

***

Mark rolled over to shut the alarm off and saw Kristen ironing. "You're an early riser."

She glanced over at him, "Good morning. Did you sleep well?"

"It's the best night's sleep I've had in a very long time. How about you?"

"Like a log."

"We should do this more often."

She gave a little laugh.

"We'll be in the car, you'll only get wrinkled again."

"It's worse than that. In a fit of self-pity last night, I just tossed everything into the suitcase. I even left my eighteen hundred dollar mint green outfit on the floor in the bathroom."

"We can stop and get it on the way to breakfast."

"Oh, I hope you don't mind, but I ordered breakfast in the room. It should be here shortly."

"I don't mind at all. A hotel without room service is like roughing it in a tent."

Kristen smiled. "A man after my own heart. Oh, and we'll have to sleep in separate bedrooms at my parents."

"Wait a minute, how long do you plan on staying?"

"Just tonight. Then we can get an early start in the morning."

There was a knock on the door. "Room Service."

Mark threw back the covers, sat on the edge of the bed and put on his slippers. "Don't open the door yet."

Kristen saw the scars on his back and one on his left thigh that she had felt last night.

He stood up and walked to the bureau, opened the drawer, slipped the loaded 9mm in and closed the drawer. "I'll go in the bathroom so you can open the door."

She gave him a once over.

He laughed and turned toward the bathroom, "Wicked woman."

"Nice tush."

Mark gave his butt an extra wiggle and closed the door.

She liked the way his broad shoulders tapered to a trim waist accenting the slender line of his hips. She'd ask him about the scars another time.

After a very brief shower and brushing his teeth he emerged wearing a white hotel robe that barely reached his knees.

Kristen had the breakfast set up on the table and poured two cups of coffee. "You brought slippers?"

"I never walk barefoot."

"Never?"

"It's a childhood thing that's carried over. If we stubbed our toe when we were kids and had bare feet, my mother would say, 'See, you deserved it, you don't have anything on your feet so don't cry to me.'"

"Wow, she was tough."

"Not really. Just teaching us a lesson. I think you'll like her."

"Is she coming to visit you?"

"No, we'll go visit her."

"As in, you and me?"

"And Pamela."

"Really, when?"

"You let me know when you can get some time off, preferably next April or May and we'll go. I mean, if you want to."

"I'd love to. Will I get to ride a horse?"

"Yes," he laughed.

"Does your daughter ride?"

"Yes, she has her own horse. She named it Sweetie Pie. The ranch hands aren't too happy about the name, they feel like fools when they have to call the horse in from the field where she grazes. Sometimes when we call my parents, Pam wants to talk to Sweetie Pie, so my father disguises his voice and pretends he's the horse."

Kristen laughed. "Oh, this sounds like fun. Do you have your own horse?"

"Yes, his name is Colorado, but I don't talk to him on the phone."

Kristen laughed and choked on the coffee.

Mark reached over and took Kristen's hand, "You seem nervous, are you all right?"

"I'm just concerned about what you might think of me coming to your door last night. I wouldn't have, except that I know you haven't dated anyone for six years. And I haven't dated anyone for two. I felt there was something going on between us and I didn't want to just walk away."

"Kristen, I knew when I opened the door and you were standing there, if you weren't really interested, you would never have come."

"I just got so upset when you said good night and walked away from me."

"Darlin', I had all I could do to make it to the elevator without going to pieces. I was just thankful there was no one in it. Let's get ready to go, we'll stop by your room and get your million dollar green thing and head to Virginia."

"It didn't cost a million dollars," she laughed.

"No, but you looked like a million dollars in it."

Kristen stood on her tiptoes and kissed Mark's cheek. "Thank you." *Okay, maybe I will wear it again.*

He patted her lovingly on the butt. "You take the bathroom first while I unload the gun and pack my gear. And remember, I'm driving."

"Mark, what would you have done... I mean, how would you have reached out to me if I didn't come to your room last night?"

"Sweetheart, I had just stepped out of the shower and was getting ready to go to your room. Begging was on my agenda."

# Chapter Three

"We made good time. I told my parents we'd be here around five o'clock."

"Is there anything else I should know about your dad before we get there?"

"I don't think so. We'll only be with them a few hours, then it's off to sleep and we'll be up and out early. We're almost there. Turn left just ahead. The driveway is beyond the gate between the two granite columns. You can pull up to the gate. When the guard sees me, he'll open... Oh, there it goes, just pull through."

The guard stepped out of the small guardhouse and walked to the driver's door. "Hello, Miss Miller. I didn't expect to see you in the passenger seat. It's good to see you."

"How have you been, Walter?"

"Not bad, gettin' old."

"Walter, this is my friend, Captain Mark Winslow, he's a detective with the NYPD."

"Well, nice to meet you, Captain Winslow."

"Thank you, Walter. What department were you with?"

Walter laughed, "Oh, I see she already told you I'm a retired cop."

"No sir, I could tell by the way you carried yourself."

Kristen bet that Walter suddenly stood six inches taller. "Well, we better be on our way, my parents are holding dinner for us."

Walter reached in the open window and gave Mark's shoulder a friendly squeeze, then stepped back.

The house was at the end of a gravel driveway that looked to be a mile long. Massive oak trees lined each side; the branches had grown across forming an arch, like a tunnel, preventing a full view of the house. An island of grass with a massive fountain blocked the center of a wide staircase in the middle of the porch that dominated the front of the house.

"Just pull around the fountain and park. You can leave the keys in the ignition. Steve will park it in the garage after Roland takes our luggage out."

"Steve and Roland?" Mark chuckled, as he pulled up in front of the massive staircase, popped the trunk and walked around the car to open Kristen's door.

Suddenly, a man dressed in jeans and a T-shirt came running toward them, "Well, my eyes must be deceiving me, could this be Counselor Miller gracing us with her presence?" The man grabbed Kristen and swung her around.

"Steve," Kristen shrieked, "put me down, I'm not ten anymore."

"You can say that again, you've either aged or put on weight."

Mark walked to the trunk to retrieve his gun case, wondering who the hell this character was.

"Don't let him bother you," the man gathering the luggage from the trunk whispered to Mark. "He's the gardener and doesn't stand a chance in hell. You'll know how important he is when she doesn't introduce you to him. But I didn't say that. My name's Roland, I'm the butler. Well, that's my title. Actually, I'm the jerk of all trades around here. Steve just wants a chance to get in the house. But I didn't say that. If you slip that gun case under my arm, I'll see that it's put in your room."

Kristen caught her breath and turned to look for Mark.

Steve cleared his throat, nervously. "I'll get out of your way, I'm sure your parents are anxious to see you. Oh, Roland, let me help you with the luggage."

"No thanks, Steve, I'm two steps away from the porch, I think you can see I've got it."

Kristen and Mark started up the staircase. "This place looks like an Antebellum Mansion. How many rooms does it have?"

"Thirty-seven, not including the servants' quarters on the third floor. My father inherited it from his father, and so on all the way back to before the Civil War."

Eight massive white pillars supported the wide porch that had ten rocking chairs on it, five on each side of the immense hand carved double oak doors. The pillars continued up to the second floor balcony and further upward to the peaked roof overhang.

They walked through the open doors into a large foyer.

The butler had already been up the stairs with the luggage and was just coming down a staircase that Mark thought had to have been designed by an architectural genius. It curved from the first floor up to the second floor, as though floating, not braced-up with supports. Each step was carpeted in the center with white, deep pile pads to protect the wide planks that matched the highly polished foyer floor.

"I put your suitcase upstairs, Miss Kristen. Welcome home."

"Thank you. It's good to be home. Roland Reynolds, this is my friend, Mark Winslow. He'll be staying in the Brown room. And we'll be leaving very early tomorrow morning."

"I already met him when you were busy with Steve. And I already put his luggage in the Brown room. Mr. Winslow, would you like me to unpack it for you?"

"That won't be necessary, but thank you."

"I put your gun case in the left hand desk drawer. Here's the key. Miss Kristen, I believe your parents are in the Library."

"Roland, do you know what time Dottie plans to serve dinner?"

"She didn't say."

"Would you let her know we're here and ask how long before dinner is served?"

"If it's going to be a little while, would you like me to bring a snack for you?"

Kristen laughed, "You know me too well." She reached for Mark's hand, "I'll introduce you to my parents now. And just so you know, it doesn't matter what time Dottie plans dinner. If she says 6:00, my father will say 6:15. He likes to think he's in charge."

Mark stopped to admire the American Civil War painting by Mark Waud.

"These paintings have hung there since I was a little girl. I never really looked at them. Are you interested in art?"

"I paint in oils, it's a hobby."

"Oh, I'd love to see some of your work."

"I'd love to show them to you," he smiled. "They're hanging on every wall in the house, including the bathrooms. I did paint one on commission, sold it for a tidy sum."

Kristen stopped walking and smiled at Mark. "I am really impressed."

Mark felt self-conscious and changed the subject. “This floor is beautiful.” The highly polished, hand hewn, wide planks set in place with woods pegs had to have been here since the house was built.

Kristen stopped and tapped on a door then entered the large library without waiting for an invite. The walls were covered, floor to ceiling, with books. Barnes & Noble came to Mark’s mind. Comfortable upholstered chairs were placed here and there.

An attractive, slender woman wearing a tailored beige dress and pearls, turned and ran to embrace her daughter. “Kris, no one told me you had arrived. Oh, it’s so good to see you. And this must be...”

“Mom, this is Mark Winslow.”

Mark could see the resemblance. He reached to shake Mrs Miller’s hand.

“I’m sorry, Mark, but I like hugs.”

“Well, so do I.” He smiled, and wrapped her in his arms to give her a hug.

“Unhand my wife, young man,” Senator Miller bellowed, jovially.

“Just keep hugging me,” Mrs Miller whispered. “He’ll want to hug Kristen anyway.” Mrs Miller gave Mark another squeeze then stood back. “My goodness, you’re tall. Well, Kristen’s tall, it makes for good hugging.” Mrs Miller tittered.

Mark smiled.

Senator Miller had his arm around Kristen’s shoulders. “Dad, this is Mark Winslow.”

The senator was a tall, heavy set man, with snow-white hair, a friendly face and a booming voice.

Mark stepped forward and extended his hand to Senator Miller. "It's a pleasure to meet you, sir."

"The pleasure is mine, Mark. Please call me Edward. And my wife's name is Marlene. Would you join me in a drink before dinner, while you ponder what the hell you've gotten yourself into?"

"If you're having one, I'll join you."

"Come on in and sit down. Name your poison."

"Whatever you're having is fine with me."

"Oh, a diplomat." Edward smiled, then walked toward the mammoth bar at the end of the room. It looked like it had been transported from an old Wild West saloon, and even had a highly polished brass foot rail from end to end. *No spittoons*, Mark thought with a chuckle.

"Kristen mentioned, when she called to tell us you were joining her, that you're a captain with the New York Police Department. Been a captain very long?" Edward held up a glass and poured a healthy amount of Scotch.

"About five-and-a-half years. I was a sheriff in Phillipsburg, Montana, back when I lived on the family ranch."

"Phillipsburg, that's in the Rocky Mountains, if I'm not mistaken. What kind of ranch, horses, cattle?"

"Angus beef, mostly. Some horses."

"Small ranch?"

"Four thousand acres."

"Now, *that's* a ranch. What happened, what made you leave that life?"

"Actually, my wife and son were killed in an auto accident. I needed a change."

Edward looked at Mark. "I'm very sorry to hear that. What happened?"

Kristen spoke up. "Dad, no need to discuss that now."

"Oh, okay. Sorry. Is that the kind of ranch that Marlene and I would want to go to, you know, a dude ranch?"

Mark recognized the questions for what they were. Edward had done a quick check on him and now he was double-checking. *Two can play at the same game. I suppose I'd do the same thing if Pamela ever brings a guy home.* "It's not a dude ranch, but we'd love to have you. You just say the word. Matter of fact, you don't have to wait for me to be there. You'd like my folks. My father is a retired Texas Ranger." Mark looked at Marlene. "It's a big ranch with plenty of room for guests. And they do love company."

"Well, by God, we might just take you up on that. I've always thought about owning a ranch. I suppose every male, at some time in his life, dreams of being a cowboy. I think I'd like the cowboy life. Is there a horse there that would be able to take my weight?"

"We have many horses to choose from."

"Are you part owner, or just going to inherit?"

"I'm part owner. My sister, Gail, and her husband, Kirk, run it for us. I had a brother, Tom, who was part owner, but he was killed in the service; a fighter pilot."

"I'm sorry to hear that. So you were married. Any children?"

"Yes, I have a daughter, Pamela. She's six years old."

Edward grinned ear to ear. "Girls, they make life worth living. Where is she now?"

"She stays with her maternal grandparents when I travel or work a lot of hours."

"Do they live on the ranch?"

"No, they live on the Connecticut coast. Most of the time she lives with me."

"Connecticut? Don't you have to live in Manhattan if you're on the force there?"

"Within a certain radius of Manhattan. I have a house in New Rochelle."

Just then, Roland knocked on the open door and entered the library. "Dinner will be served in half an hour."

"Oh, is that so?" Edward bellowed. "We'll have dinner when I decide to eat, and not when Dottie decides that I'm hungry."

"Dad," Kristen interrupted his verbal tirade, "I asked Roland to ask Dottie."

"Oh, sorry," Edward muttered and quickly turned to pour more drinks.

"I brought a snack for you just in case." Roland placed the tray of finger sandwiches near Mark. He knew the liquor would be flowing and the food would help.

Kristen thanked the butler then turned and smiled at Mark. "Dad rules the roost, but the cook rules the rooster, even though he'll never admit it." She smiled at her father, then looked at Mark. "We'll have time for one more quick drink and then we can freshen up for dinner."

"Mark, we could take our drinks and sit over here in what I call my inner sanctum." Edward indicated an alcove at the end of the library near the bar. The alcove had three wide steps leading down to it. Behind the bar, five windows, or maybe French doors, reached from floor to ceiling.

"Edward, why don't you both sit over here opposite Kristen and me? You can't keep Mark all to yourself." Marlene indicated the matching couch opposite her, which flanked a fieldstone fireplace large enough for a man to stand up in. Not being the season for a rip-roaring fire, it was decorated with potted plants.

"Or we can sit with Marlene and Kristen. Come on, Mark, I knew she'd say that."

Mark laughed, "I know what you mean. I had planned to fly home from Atlanta and do some painting in my house this weekend, but you see where I ended up."

Mark reached for a sandwich.

"I hope you didn't insist that Mark..."

"No, Mom," Kristen laughed. "Believe me, if he didn't want to be here, he wouldn't." Kristen noticed that Mark wasn't touching his drink. "And, Caped Crusader, now that you got me in trouble with my mother, would you add a little water to my drink? I'm afraid if I drink this on an empty stomach I won't be a fit dinner partner."

Mark gratefully took her glass, knowing she was giving him a chance to water down his own drink.

"Let me ask you a question, Mark. You're a captain, right?"

"Yes."

"I thought captains sat around the station telling people what to do. How is it you're out working on these rape cases?"

Mark smiled. *So he's really been checking on me.* "I've had extensive training and experience in serial rapists. When we couldn't catch a break on these two perps, it was decided by the big wigs that I'd be a working captain."

"I'd say that's putting it rather humbly. After dinner I'll take you on in a game of billiards. Do you play?"

"A little," Mark lied. He'd won a few tournaments in his day. And had a regulation size pool table in his basement playroom.

"You can include me in on that, only we'll play for money."

"Oh no you don't. Watch her, Mark, she could beat the pants off of Fats what's his name."

"Minnesota Fats," Marlene assisted.

"Another pool expert heard from. I'm telling you, Mark, I don't stand a chance around here with these two..."

Kristen looked at her watch. "Perhaps we could continue this conversation during dinner. I'll show Mark to his room. We'll freshen up and meet you in the dining room in fifteen minutes."

Kristen closed the library door, slipped her arm through Marks's arm and smiled up at him. Walking up the stairs, she said, "I can see I'm going to have one hell of a time trying to share you with my father while we're here."

"Make an appointment with my secretary," Mark teased, "and I'll try to find time to squeeze you in."

Kristen laughed then lovingly gripped his hand. "This is your room. In case you get lost, it's the second door on the left at the top of the stairs."

"Where's your room?"

She pointed to her bedroom door. "This just happens to be conveniently across the hall from your room."

Mark put his arm around Kristen's shoulders and turned to enter his room. He was surprised to see a towering four-poster king size bed at the far end. "How many people are going to live in here with me?"

Kristen laughed, "Only me, but just for a while. So don't lock your door when we come back upstairs."

"You better bring a flag to wave so I can find you in that bed. Then after you have your way with me, you'll have to go back to your room, because I don't like to be crowded when I sleep."

Kristen tried to stop laughing.

"Where's the bathroom?"

"Oh, it's through that door. Every bedroom has its own bathroom. If you need anything, just dial nine on the house phone on the desk."

"What could I possibly need?"

"I'll come back and get you or you'll never find the dining room."

"You mean, I actually have to walk somewhere, dinner isn't delivered?"

"Oh, if you want to eat in the room, yes it will..."

"I was only kidding."

"Oh. Well, I'll come back in about ten minutes. Is that enough time for you?"

"Plenty."

Kristen stepped into the hall and closed the door.

Mark headed for the bathroom. It was the size of his living room at home. In the center of the room sat a huge copper, claw foot, slipper tub. He looked in to see how deep it was. *That would fit a family of four.* Then he wondered if the high-tank toilet on the far wall really worked. He pulled the chain to give it a test drive, and noticed his toiletries had been unpacked and set out neatly beside a pedestal sink that was large enough to float a row boat.

# Chapter Four

"There's the skyline, we're finally home," Kristen said, happily. She sat up, straightened her clothes and finger combed her hair. Glancing at the clock on the dashboard, "Oh, no wonder I'm tired, it's four in the morning."

"What are you tired from?" Mark laughed and mussed her hair with his hand. "I did all the driving."

"That's your own fault, you didn't want me to drive."

"No, I wanted to get here in one piece."

"Well, I'm tired from trying to keep you awake," Kristen teased.

"Oh, is that right? The only thing you did to keep me awake was snore loud." Mark smiled and placed his hand on her knee. "I'm hungry. Let's find a diner and have an early breakfast."

"We could have breakfast at my place."

"Sounds good to me, I'm starving."

"Do you want me to set the GPS so you can find the apartment building?"

Mark looked at her, "Uh, I'm a New York cop, I think I can find a building. Matter of fact, I know exactly where it is."

"Oh, pardon me for stepping all over your ego. What time did it start raining?" She exaggerated a stretch, then yawned. "I must have dozed off for a minute or two."

"Or three," he laughed. "It started raining about two hours ago and I call that more than just dozing off."

"Manhattan — love it or get the hell out, there's no in-between. This is about the only time the streets are empty, except for an occasional car or pedestrian. All the homeless are safely tucked away in their cardboard boxes, and no push-cart hot dog stands on every corner."

PREPARE TO TURN RIGHT, TURN RIGHT HERE.

"Just pull close to the security phone on the wall. It's voice recognition so I'll have to speak into it..."

As if to prove her right, the steel door blocking the entrance to the garage under her hi-rise apartment building opened electronically. Mark drove in. The steel door shut behind them.

"Do you have an assigned parking place?"

"Yes, there are two. One for my father when he comes to visit or entertains a few dignitaries. Look on the right for spaces twenty-three and twenty-four."

Mark parked the car in the space marked twenty-three and popped the trunk. "I'll get your luggage, since you didn't bring Roland with us to carry it in."

"Roland hates New York."

"Smart man," Mark mumbled under his breath. "It was nice of your father to let you use his Lincoln."

Kristen smiled as she removed her overnight case from the trunk. "He wasn't doing me a favor. He just likes to drive my Corvette. I think he's having a late mid-life crisis. The elevator is over here. The apartment is on the sixteenth floor."

Mark pushed the button with his elbow. "Is that your stomach rumbling, or mine?"

"I think it's both," she laughed and unlocked her apartment door.

"Where do you want this suitcase?"

"Just set it there beside the overnight case. I don't like clutter in the bedroom. The maid will take care of them in the morning. I'm starved. How about a full breakfast?"

"You have a maid?"

"Well, not exactly a maid. She's more a housekeeper. She lives upstairs in my friend Carol's apartment and comes down here once a day. I don't like to do dishes or... She does my laundry and changes my bed. Dusts. Things like that. Do you want a tour of the apartment before breakfast or after?"

"How much does the tour cost?"

Kristen gave a little laugh, "One kiss."

"I can afford that, but one kiss is my limit."

"Okay, but you have to pay in advance."

"Oh no. First I want to know if the tour is worth it."

"Then follow me, but you better pay up as soon as the tour is finished or you won't get any breakfast."

Mark rubbed his hands together and grinned. "Oh, I can't wait to see what that will cost me."

"We'll start here at the bar."

"It's a smaller version of your father's bar in Virginia." *Fully stocked with nothing but the best.* Mark noticed a bottle of Marquis de Montesquiou 1904 Vintage Armagnac. *That goes for somewhere between six and seven thousand bucks, closer to seven. I thought only my uncle stocked that.*

Kristen pointed toward the ceiling, "This is an antique glass rack my father had installed shortly after I moved in."

"Very impressive. It's stocked better than any bar I've been in."

Kristen smiled and took his hand, "Let's hurry right along, we don't want to bump into any crowds during this tour. This is the kitchen," she indicated needlessly as they walked into a spotless galley with a menagerie of well-used pots, wire whisks, nested stainless steel bowls, ladles and colanders in every shape, color and size.

"Can you cook?"

"Very little and only if I have to."

"How little?"

"As little as possible."

"You certainly have every appliance imaginable. And a collection of cookbooks." Mark chose one from a selection of approximately thirty. FANCY PASTRIES. "Have you ever made any of these?"

"Oh sure. I try a different one each time there's a party and I'm asked to bring something."

"Really?"

"Yes. Then I trash it and stop at the bakery on the way."

Mark laughed, the sound filling the kitchen. He gave her a hug and then stood back, keeping his hands on her shoulders. Looking very serious, "Can you make meatloaf? It's my favorite."

"Oh, I make a great meatloaf, even if I do say so myself. I'll make one for you sometime."

"I'd like that," he grinned. "Shall we continue the tour?"

"The only problem is you need a chainsaw to slice it. The outside of my meatloaf has often been referred to as bark, as in tree bark. But once you get into the middle of it..." She laughed, teasingly and hurried toward the door at the opposite end of the kitchen.

Mark quickly followed her into a formal dining room. "What do you serve in here, peanut butter and jelly sandwiches?" He looked around admiring the massive furniture. "This is beautiful."

"Do you really like it? My father hates it, says it's too formal. I bought the furniture at an auction in a castle in England. Some poor duke was defrocked, or whatever it's called when a duke loses his shirt. While it was being shipped over, which took six whole months, I had the dining room decorated to create the proper setting. A seamstress came in and made the red velvet drapes to match the chair cushions." Kristen walked to the window, pressed a button and the drapes closed. "I had to have this electric curtain rod installed, because the drapes are so heavy."

Mark pulled a chair away from the table and sat down. "No wonder it took six months, this chair must weigh a hundred pounds." He tried to lift the table, and then looked up at the massive crystal chandelier. "Who keeps that sparkling?"

"Certainly not me," Kristen laughed. "My father says it's ostentatious."

"I don't think so, it fits the dining room perfectly. Anything smaller would look paltry in comparison to everything else in the room. What castle did you get that out of?"

"I designed it and then had it made."

Mark looked at her in surprise. "That is beautiful. You amaze me. Just don't tell me the price, it's probably my year's salary."

"Oh, good heaven's no," she laughed. "It wasn't that much, but my father had a fit when I told him the price."

Mark stood up, wrestled the chair back into place, and then stepped to a massive sideboard, decorated with what he guessed to be antiques. A small Florentine silver frame grabbed his attention. Kristen was standing beside a young man. "Is this Richard?"

"Yes, that's the day we announced our engagement. Do you want to finish this tour?"

"Not just yet. I'd like to know about Richard. Do you miss him or visit his grave? I'm just wondering if..."

"No, Mark, I don't miss him. I'm almost thankful that he died before we were married. He only dated me to get close to my father. As soon as he got access to my father, he didn't need me anymore. Oh, he pretended to care in front of others. I was devastated, crushed, embarrassed at my stupidity, mainly for having ignored the warnings my father had always told me, 'Be sure the man you love, loves you for you and not what your father can do for him.' After Richard died I took no chances, I haven't dated anyone. And I never confided in anyone, not even Carol. I'm sure people thought I stayed alone out of respect for Richard. But it was for my safety that I refused every dinner invitation. Always in the back of my mind I'd wonder what *he* could be after other than me."

Mark placed the frame face down and took Kristen into his arms. "Are you sure about me?"

"If I wasn't I would never have gone to room six-two-zero that night." She smiled up at him.

Mark kissed her. "Let's get this tour moving."

They walked to the opposite end of the dining room and into a hall. "That's the bathroom and..."

"The bathroom?" He looked in. "You could park a bus in there."

"It's not that big," Kristen laughed and tugged on Mark's arm.

"And in there is my father's bedroom, when he comes to visit. And the other door is his office, but he keeps that locked."

"Doesn't your mother come with him?"

"Not anymore. She did a few times, but he's always so busy when he's here, she felt she might as well stay at home. And this is my bedroom." She flipped the light switch.

"Oh good, my favorite part of the tour." Mark stepped into a large, yet cozy room with an antique four-poster bed. The bedspread and drapes were over-the-top feminine — not a room a man could permanently share.

"I'd show you the walk-in closet, but the light bulb is out."

"That's okay, when you've seen one closet, you've seen them all."

"That ends the tour. Now, how about breakfast?"

Mark sat on the edge of the bed. "Come and sit down with me for a minute."

Kristen walked to where he was sitting. "What's wrong?"

"Nothing's wrong. I'm just a little concerned about us. I want to keep seeing you, but Kristen, I don't want to waste your time. Let's say we get serious, you know, down the road. I could never afford to support you in this lifestyle. This apartment must have cost you, I don't know, close to a couple of million. You're out of my league, I mean, really, Park Avenue is above my budget..."

"Mark, I thought you understood. This isn't my apartment, it's my father's. I only live here..." Kristen looked perplexed, "You thought I owned all this?"

"Well, it certainly looked that way. I mean, you decorated it, bought furniture from a castle in England, had drapes made and designed that beautiful chandelier."

"Yes. And my father paid for all of it. This apartment is where my father entertains people from the UN, and politicians from other states when they're in town. The reason I live here is that when I was engaged to Richard, he owned a house that we were going to live in. I gave my notice at my apartment that coincided with the wedding date. When Richard died I still lived in my apartment, but the lease ran out. And someone else had already signed a new lease. I had nowhere to live. And you know apartments in Manhattan are few and far between."

Mark just stared at her, trying to take it all in. "Oh, so you were almost homeless?" He grinned.

"Well, I could have lived upstairs with Carol and Joshua, if need be. Now I want to ask you something."

"You can ask me anything."

"What are the scars on your back and leg from?"

Mark hesitated. "I was shot a couple of times."

"That's more than a couple of times."

"Well, the three in the back were all the bullets he had left in his gun. The one on the leg was another time, an escaped felon, but he didn't live long enough to empty his gun. If the scars bother you..."

"No, I just wondered what happened."

"I notice you try not to touch them when we're making love."

"Oh, that's because I didn't know if it would hurt if I touched them."

Mark stood up, pulled Kristen to her feet and kissed her. "Not at all. Sometimes I forget they're there, like at the hotel, I should have worn my T-shirt."

"No, I'm glad you didn't. Well, not glad, you know what I mean."

Mark looked at her and grinned. "*You're* blushing." He could see she was embarrassed. "Come on, let's have breakfast, I'm starved. After we eat I'll call the station and get a ride home."

As they walked across the hall to the kitchen, Kristen suggested, "I could drive you home... Or you could drive and I'll go with you, that way I'll know where you live."

"That's a great idea. Since this is Saturday, why don't you pack a few things, stay overnight, and tomorrow we could drive to Connecticut and pick up Pamela. That way she'll get to meet you."

"I'd love that. Oh wait, you mean meet your in-laws?"

"I'll call and let them know the plan so they can say yes or no. But really, they're fantastic people and I'm positive there won't be a problem."

"Let's eat first and then I'll shuffle a few things around in the overnight case." Kristen was nervously excited, but was sure she could handle meeting them, though she did notice her hands were shaking when she began to prepare breakfast. "I'd ask if you want sunny-side up, easy over, or scrambled, but when I cook they end up sunny-side down, hard over, or mushy."

Mark stood next to Kristen and put his arm around her shoulders. "Why don't you go pack a few things and I'll cook the breakfast?"

Kristen smiled and handed Mark the spatula. "Whether you know it or not, you just saved your own life. Call me when it's ready."

Mark hummed while he cooked, thinking, *sunny-side down, easy over, hard over? Meatloaf with bark? We'll definitely need to hire a cook... Now where the hell did that idea come from?*

***

"Here we are."

"Mark, it's lovely. I've always wanted a white picket fence. Oh my God, I shouldn't have said that. I just meant..."

"Darlin', I know what you meant." He kissed her hand. "I'll pull into the driveway behind my car and grab the suitcases out of the trunk."

Mark popped the trunk and they walked to the back of the car.

"The house is bigger than I thought it would be. Is it a Colonial?"

"Yes, it was built in 1910, but the previous owners brought everything up to date. It has a fireplace, four bedrooms, two bathrooms and what they call a powder room, I call it a half bath. Oh, and a formal dining room that we never use. And there's a playroom and laundry room in the walk-out basement. Come on, I'll give you a tour, but it will cost..."

"There's a frumpy looking man staring at us at the end of your driveway."

Mark turned to look. "Oh, that's my neighbor. Hi, Lloyd."

"Sorry to bother you, Mark. I just wanted to let you know we're having the neighborhood gathering next weekend, sort of an end the summer party. You remember, we did it last year. All the neighbors get together, line the street with picnic tables and grills. A few kegs. There's music and games for the kids."

"I remember. It was great fun. What can I bring this year?"

"Well, the ladies will bring the food, so would a keg again this year be okay with you?"

"How about two kegs, I remember last year we ran short."

Lloyd laughed. "I forgot about that. Two would be perfect. Say, could you get some of those same plastic cups you brought last year?"

"Be glad to. Let me know if you need anything else." When Lloyd didn't turn and leave, Mark took Kristen's hand and walked the short distance to the end of the driveway to shake Lloyd's hand. "Lloyd Blanchard, this is my friend Kristen Miller."

"This is a pleasure, Kristen. Sorry to bother you folks, but it's so difficult to find Mark." He turned and started to walk away. "I hope to see you both next weekend. Now I have to go let all the looky-loos know she's not your sister." He laughed again and did a little jig with his feet.

Mark chuckled and shook his head. "Are you free next weekend?"

"I am if you want me to be, but don't feel obligated."

"I want."

"Then I'll be here."

"Good. You'll make the neighbors happy."

"Why is that?"

"They can finally stop trying to fix me up."

"Oh, then I'll definitely be here. Does Lloyd always speak in the same quiet monotone?"

"Yes. Lloyd's a genius. He's a math professor, teaches Actuarial Science. And now, my beauty, come into my lair and I'll show you my etchings."

# Chapter Five

Mark couldn't remember when he'd enjoyed the ride to work as much as this first morning back, following his trip to Atlanta. Especially, having spent the guiltless weekend alone with Kristen, after Pamela told him, "Dad, we have plans. Gramps is on vacation this week so we're going to Six Flags at Lake George for three days."

He parked his car in the lot behind the station knowing that Monday morning was not a day to go in the front door. The desk sergeant's area would hold the Saturday night miasma of vomit, sweat, unwashed bodies and moldy crotches carried there by the bong freaks, prostitutes, drug aficionados and fermented drunks until at least next Friday, and then fortify itself again on Saturday night.

Hurrying through the maze to the locker room, he saw his partner, Sergeant Lewis. "Dave, can you get our crew together in the Squad Room for oh-nine-hundred and call me when you're ready?"

"What's up?"

Mark looked at him. "Did you say something?"

"I said, what's up, meaning what do you want me to bring with me, what should I be ready for?"

"Sorry Dave, my mind is galloping like a stallion after its mare. I just want to bring everyone up to date. I'll be in my office organizing the pile of updates that I'm sure is on my desk."

Mark quickly exchanged his weapons, placing his personal SIG Sauer 9mm in his locker. Checking that his service weapon was loaded and the safety was on, he slipped it into the leather holster under his left arm, then headed to his office through the labyrinth of welcome-back greetings. Just as he thought, his desk was a shambles.

***

"Good morning, everyone." He waited until there was silence. "Just a couple of things to bring you up to date while the long days turn into weeks and the weeks into months. We're positive we're looking for two men. I guess that's a given by now. So far we don't have anyone we're even remotely interested in. All the fingerprints and blood match the victims. There's absolutely no DNA from the suspects."

While Mark made his report he was careful to look at the eyes of each man and woman in his crew, randomly selecting the next person, but careful to touch on all of them. He had found that looking at their eyes, rather than the tops of their heads while talking, held their attention.

"The first victim was a court reporter. The second victim was a forensic psychologist. The third attack was a social worker. And the fourth attack was a woman who was attending the police academy. She survived, but just barely."

He waited for the whispers to cease. "She had a female roommate, a nurse who works the nightshift who wasn't home at the time. The first three, I think, represent the court system. The fourth victim, the cadet, may represent a police officer who they hoped did not have a weapon." He waited for the murmurs to cease.

"We've cleared family and friends of the victims. I thank all of you for your diligence in clearing them while I was on, as you all know, a forced three day R&R in delightful downtown muggy Atlanta.

Our forensic psychologist reports that considering the victims' professions, one or both of these guys have been in more than one of our previous line-ups. We've probably had our hands on them at one time or another. By that I mean New York, not just this precinct. One is more than likely the leader, a sadistic psychopath who will usually have a follower. Also, this is mission oriented, a vendetta, very focused and with a plan. They're careful to wait until there's only one person, the victim, home alone at night. And the psycho and his schizo pal will wait as long as it takes to get the victim alone. They know who they're after. They bring their own torture instruments so there isn't a household knife or tool used that we could get DNA or a fingerprint from. They're most likely wearing rubber gloves.

The rope used to tie the victim is standard clothesline, very old so we don't know where or when it was purchased.

These two maggots are going to hit again multiple times before we get a lead, but they will make a mistake eventually.

A heads-up has been sent to female court employees, social workers and academy cadets. Hopefully, the media will keep everyone else on their toes.

It took a few weeks before the cadet was strong enough to give us a description and to work with the sketch artist. We released the sketch, which generated thousands of calls. One caller said he'd seen a person many times who looks like the sketch, but he can't remember where he saw him. So we've got the usual do-gooders who don't know shit from Shinola.

Somewhere there's a teacher, a counselor, a relative or friend who knows one of these characters and was aware there was something strange about him. Hopefully, something will click.

This is a nightmare and we're all getting frustrated, but it's the next victim we have to be concerned about. Sooner or later we will zero in on these two.

All time off and/or vacations are canceled unless medical or bereavement or you've already booked something expensive, but clear it with me even if it's already on the schedule."

When the moaning simmered down, Mark announced, "Officer James Yussif, I'll see *you* in my office.

I want all of you to grab a few calls and hit the pavement. Be safe."

Mark gathered his notes and headed to his office, trying not to make eye contact with anyone who would want to start a conversation. He sat in his squeaky desk chair and thought about putting his feet up on the desk.

"You wanted to see me?"

"Yes, Jim. Come in, have a seat. We have a complaint about you threatening to deck an old woman yesterday."

"Now wait a minute, I didn't threaten her."

"The woman says you did. And the woman is the mayor's aunt."

"Oh shit."

"It's worse than that. What happened?"

"I didn't threaten her," he yelled.

"Calm down, start at the beginning and don't pound my desk again."

"We narrowed down four people who had called-in, who sounded legitimate, saying they had seen a suspicious person in their building. Two of them were women so I asked Officer Balofino to go with me."

"Samantha Balofino?"

"Yes. When we got done interviewing two of the four people, we were standing in the hall waiting for the elevator and this old lady came out of her apartment and began telling us about some guy she saw in the hall who she didn't recognize."

Officer Yussif removed a small notebook from his pocket and began reading his notes. "I asked when this happened. She told me it was about 3:30 in the morning. I asked if we could talk to her in her apartment. We went in and sat down. She started telling us a story and then would go off on another tangent.

Sam kept getting her back to the original story. After a half hour or so, I began to suspect the woman didn't know anything, she just wanted someone to talk to. You know how some of them get."

"Yes. Unfortunately, I do."

"So I asked her why she had been in the hallway at 3:30 in the morning. And she told me, in no uncertain terms, that she had already explained to me that she was emptying her trash. She said, 'I'm old, old people sleep in spurts. There's no day or night for us, like you young scalawags have. We sleep when we're tired."

Mark was trying to keep a straight face.

"She went on to explain how it could be a two hour nap, then up for a few hours, then another nap.

Then she said, 'So anyway, back to the crime scene, I was walking toward the trash chute...'"

"She actually said, so back to the crime scene?"

"Yes. Then she said, 'I don't know why they put the trash chute so far away from my apartment. It's way down by the elevators at the other end of the hall.' Then she said, 'Well, I suppose, when the place was built, they didn't know I'd be moving in three years later.'

So, I interrupted her. Frankly, I was losing my patience. It was the tenth time one of us had to get her back to the subject and we had other people to interview. I said, Ma'am, you saw someone you didn't recognize in the hall... And she said," — checking his notes again — "'Oh yes. Well, when he turned and saw me, he quickly turned and pretended he was waiting for the elevator. And that's when I knew he was up to no good.' So I asked her, How did you know that? And she said, 'Well, if he had been waiting for the elevator to come to the floor, the call button, you know, the small panel beside the door with two buttons, you push the bottom one to call the elevator and it lights up. Well, it wasn't lit. And that's how I knew he was only pretending to wait for the elevator. But I didn't let on, I just smiled and went back to my apartment and locked the door.' Then I asked if she remembered what day that happened. And she said, 'Well now, let me think.' And she thought and thought. Finally, she said, 'It would have been last night. No, that's not right, it may have been...' I reminded her that she had told us she reported it to the manager and he'll have a record that we can look at.

So, Sam thanked her and we escaped, uh, I mean we left and hurried to the elevator. And I said to Sam, If she went on one more of her daffy tangents I was going to deck her."

"You were in the hallway when you said that to Sam?"

"Yes."

"Where was the woman?"

"She was in her apartment when we left. But she must have followed us, because as soon as I said it, she was right behind us and said, 'I heard that wisecrack about going to deck me.' She started shaking her fist at me and said, 'Don't you come back here to talk to me without a bodyguard. If there's any decking to be done, you'll be the one on the floor.' Sam and I got into the elevator and I panic pushed the CLOSE DOOR button."

When Mark stopped laughing, he said, "Okay, Jim, I'll take care of this. Oh, wait a minute, did you check with the manager about it?"

"Yes. He told me the guy she saw is a reclusive tenant who walks with his head down, his hands in his pockets, doesn't make eye contact, wears a black raincoat, rain or shine, and comes and goes all hours of the day and night. But that he pays his rent on time, so they don't pester him. Then the old woman reports him every time she sees him while she's out skulking the halls looking for burglars, but then she forgets that she's already reported him."

*What a goddamn waste of my time.* "Tell Sam I want to see her before the end of shift. I'll corroborate and put it on record in case we have any further bullshit about it."

"Captain, I don't mean to be a jerk about this, but could you ask Sam to come in right now. I don't want anyone to say I filled her in on what I just told you. I mean, my job could be on the line here."

"Absolutely. Good thinking. And let's keep this between the three of us. I'll give you a SEE ME NOW note to give to Sam. If I go out to the bullpen to get her, everyone will want to know why I wanted to see her, what I wanted, did I finally ask her for a date. And Jim, don't lose that notebook."

"I'll put it in my locker and start a new one. Thank you."

*He missed his calling as a court reporter.*

Later, Samantha confirmed Officer Yussif's story. Then added, "If I may say something..."

Mark looked up at her, "Yes, go ahead."

"Jim works like," she circled her hands left and right, "a mainframe going through every story. He doesn't leave anything to chance. He examines every scrap of paper. Now and then finding a detective's girlfriend's phone number and keeps it to himself, you know, private. He writes everything down and follows through with the determination of a dumpster diver."

"You don't have to answer this, but are you two romantically involved?"

"No sir. I'm engaged to one of the players on a," she winked and formed quotation marks in the air with her fingers, "'local team', but I don't tell anyone or they'll be hounding me for free tickets and signatures. You may have heard of him on the news, because everyone thinks his partner's name is Sam." She could still hear Captain Winslow laughing when she got back to her desk.

# Chapter Six

Kristen sat on the blanket and watched Mark, in his dark blue swim trunks, playing with his six-year-old daughter, Pamela. She looked so cute in a pink bathing suit, making endless trips from the ocean, with plastic pails filled with water, to the moat surrounding the sand castle they had just built. The sand absorbed the water faster than they could pour. Even the flag, made out of a Popsicle stick and its wrapper, kept tipping over.

Mark ran back and forth four times to Pamela's half-trip. Her bare feet dimpled the soft sand with every step as she hurried to keep up with her father. Half of her bounty would spill out before she could add it to Mark's futile attempt at filling the hand-made trough of thirsty sand.

"I think you should give that up as a lost cause," Kristen sympathized.

"I think we should have built it closer to the water so we didn't have to run so far," he replied, as he fell spread-eagle on the sand in defeat.

"The tide was in when you made it. Now it's going out."

"Come on, Daddy, we have to fill the moat."

"Pumpkin, we can't fill it. I'm exhausted, and the water is freezing my ankles."

Pamela turned to smile at Kristen. Then, without warning, poured the cold water onto Mark's back.

Mark roared at the shock and quickly got to his feet. Pamela was ready to run, but was momentarily transfixed waiting to see if her dad was really angry or fooling. He smiled and started after her. Pamela ran a straight path, jumping over people, towels, cameras, and running across blankets. Mark took the long, polite way around. Pamela was running and laughing, losing ground every time she turned to see how close he was to actually catching her. She suddenly turned and ran back toward their blanket to hide behind Kristen.

"Hide me."

Kristen quickly threw a towel over Pamela's head. "Here he comes, stay still," she whispered.

Mark pretended he couldn't see his daughter half hidden under a towel. "Where is she, did you see which way she went?"

"Who?"

Mark dropped to his knees in the sand, laughing. "I don't know who is worse, you or Pamela." He crawled to the blanket. "We might as well eat lunch while she's gone. I'll eat her dessert first."

"Wait a minute!" Pamela shouted, as she threw off the towel. "I'm right here and Gram made that dessert special for me."

After they ate, Kristen packed away the lunch things and gathered the trash in a small bag.

Mark collected the pails and shovels, rinsed the water toys in the ocean and stuffed them into the large cloth bag.

"Mark, if you'll rinse Pamela's feet and then carry her here to the blanket, I'll dry them and she can put her sneakers on."

When everything was together, Mark and Kristen shook the blanket and folded it.

"It was a nice day,' Kristen smiled.

"A good way to end the summer," Mark added. "Alice will probably have tea and dessert ready by now. And Henry will be home from work shortly."

"Daddy, I'm going to run ahead to Gram's. I can see her on the porch."

"Okay. Tell her we're on our way."

"I will," she yelled, as she ran along the sandy path to her maternal grandparents' cottage.

Mark held Kristen's hand, "Thank you for coming today. I know it must have been difficult for you."

"A little. But I'm sure it was more distressing for Alice to see someone else with you. Realizing that really helped me to hide my jitters. Your mother-in-law is very nice. I was a little worried that she wouldn't accept me as graciously as she did. She is really lovely."

Turning to Kristen, he pulled her gently to him. "You are one fantastic lady. Not many women would even try to accept Alice and Henry as part of my family." He leaned down and kissed her.

"Hey, you two love birds," Alice called to them from the screened porch on the back of the cottage, "dessert is ready."

Mark waved, "We're coming, Alice."

Henry stepped out of the kitchen door and put his arm around his wife. Alice snuggled into him. "Mark has a phone call, so be prepared, he may have to leave immediately." And, he smiled to himself, *he may have to leave Pamela here.* "Mark, there's a Dave Lewis on the phone, says it's important. He couldn't get through on your cell so he called the house."

"That's my partner, it must be important for him to call me here." Mark and Kristen started to run to the house. Mark took the stairs two at a time and ran inside.

"Kristen, this is my husband, Henry. He just got home from work."

"Well," Henry greeted Kristen, "you're even prettier than Mark described."

"Thank you, Mr. Clark." Kristen blushed. "And thank you both for accepting me into your home. I was a little nervous, to say the least, when Mark told me we'd be driving to Connecticut, for Pamela's last visit before school starts."

"We're pleased you would come. It may be uncomfortable for all of us at first, but it's for Pamela's and Mark's benefit that we at least try. Don't you agree?"

"Most definitely."

"Mark is very special to us and we're just so thrilled that he's found happiness with you." Alice tried to hide her emotions. "Shall we have tea and dessert while Mark's on the phone? We always have tea when Henry gets home from work. And today I made strawberry shortcake. It's Mark's favorite."

"Gram, I'm going to go sit with daddy while he's on the phone."

Kristen knew a six year old should not hear what Mark was discussing. "Pamela, would you mind staying with me at this table, we can tell your grandparents how we tricked daddy this afternoon."

Henry caught on to the ruse, "What's this, you were able to trick your dad?"

Pamela grinned, "Yup, we did, Gramps."

"No, you couldn't have. No one can ever trick him."

"Yes, Gramps, I did. And Kristen helped. Daddy was on the sand and I dumped..." Pamela went on and on, barely taking a breath.

Henry was laughing and kept asking questions to keep Pamela from hearing her dad on the phone.

"Gram, since I already ate my lunch and my dessert before, can I have ice cream now?"

"Absolutely, if you'll eat it out on the porch."

Alice served Pamela her ice cream and returned to the table. "There, that will give us a chance to talk privately. Kristen, we're very pleased that Mark will be re-marrying, especially now that we've met you..."

"Mark hasn't said anything to me about marriage."

"Oh, he hasn't said anything to us, either," Alice lied, "but he's never brought anyone here before, so we just assumed..." *Oh my, now I've done it.*

"Alice, if it's that important to you, please go on. We'll keep it to ourselves, just in case."

Alice took a deep breath. "What I'm trying to say is, if you and Mark get married, we hope that we'll still be allowed to see Pamela. We are her grandparents and..."

"There's no need to say anymore. I promise that I will never come between you and Pamela. I think it's very important for Pamela to continue in the same family relationship that she has with you now. And if we do get married and have children, I hope you'll be their grandparents, also."

"Mark's coming." Henry whispered.

"Hey, what's going on out here, a powwow?"

"Oh good, you're off the phone," Alice said, wiping a tear from her eye. "I made strawberry shortcake for dessert."

"My favorite." Mark leaned down to kiss Alice on the cheek. "You're too good to me."

"More problems, Mark?" Henry asked. "Was that about the case you're working on?"

"I'm afraid so." He'd keep the gruesome details to himself of another woman raped using a broken bottle and left for dead. "As soon as we have the shortcake we'll have to leave." He didn't want to hurt his mother-in-law's feelings by not eating it.

"There have been seven incidents, that we know of, by the same two rapists and we still have absolutely nothing to go on; no clues, no set pattern. I wouldn't be surprised if we had them in our grasp at one time or another, but didn't link them with anything."

"Well, I'm sure you'll catch them," Henry smiled.

Mark looked at his watch. "We have to get going. Can you keep Pamela for a few days?"

"We already planned to, when you got the phone call."

"Thank you. I'll gather our things and go out and say goodbye to Pamela."

Mark kissed his mother-in-law on the cheek. "Thank you for everything."

Alice held onto Mark and whispered, "I think I let the cat out of the bag while you were on the phone. You told me you were going to propose on the beach. What happened?"

"I wanted to get her alone. I was just going to ask her while we were walking back to the house, but all hell broke loose when I got the phone call. Then I thought I'd take her to dinner tonight, but I might not get the chance. I'll ask her later tonight."

Mark went out to the porch and hugged Pamela. "I'm sorry, but I got a call."

"I know, Dad. Don't worry, I like staying with gram and gramps." She smiled and went back to her coloring book.

"I'll try to get back tomorrow or the next day."

Mark popped the trunk and threw their wet bathing suits and towels in, then waved goodbye and they headed back to New York.

"Pamela reminded me that she starts school next week and asked if I could pick her up if you didn't get the chance. I said I would. Is that okay with you?"

"Of course it is. You don't have to ask. It would really be a big help to me. And we have that neighborhood get-together this coming weekend. I did ask Pamela if she'd like to stay with Alice and Henry and start school there."

"What did she say?"

"She said no. That she likes staying with them as long as she knows she'll be going home. To quote word for word, 'No, I like visiting here as long as I know you'll always come back and get me.'"

Kristen grabbed a tissue and dabbed at her eyes, "Sorry, but sometimes she just grabs my heart and squeezes."

"You should have seen me when she said it. I had to hug her for five minutes and dig my thumbnail into my palm."

Kristen dozed off, as usual, for most of the ride.

"Sweetheart, wake up we're almost there. I'll drop you at your place. If I get a chance I'll come back rather than go home. Is that okay with you?"

"Of course, just give me a heads-up so I can get rid of the boyfriend."

Mark laughed and messed her hair. "The doorman won't recognize you."

"Do I look that bad?" She tried to finger comb her hair.

Mark pulled up to the curb. "I'll see you later."

"Okay. You've got your own key, just try not to wake me."

"Do you think you can sleep through me having my way with you?"

Kristen smirked, "Yes, I do it all the time."

"What if I bring Chinese food, would you want me to wake you for that?"

"Definitely yes. I could wait up if you're bringing Chinese."

Mark laughed, "I think I'll trade you in."

"Okay, but after the Chinese food." Kristen kissed him and got out of the car.

***

The house phone rang. Kristen answered on the first ring, "Hi".

"How did you know it was me?"

"Because no one else would dare call me at two thirty in the morning."

"I'm on my way."

"I'm waiting...in the nightgown you bought for me."

Mark blared the siren once.

Kristen laughed and hung up the phone. She hurried to the kitchen and set out serving spoons, two plates and two Chinese tea cups. Then hurried to put the kettle on to boil and ran to the door to watch through the peephole so Mark wouldn't have to struggle with the key while holding the food. She knew he'd be furious if she waited with the door open.

Mark walked to the door and tapped, knowing she'd be standing on the opposite side.

Kristen swung the door open. "Do you want to eat before or after?

He looked at her and saw her ice blue eyes dancing with the same emotions that he was feeling. "After is..."

"Good, that's what I thought." She grabbed the bag of food, carried it to the kitchen, turned off the kettle and hurried to the bedroom.

Mark was almost undressed.

"I bought the CD you wanted, it's in the player. Why did you want 'Ravel's Bolero?'"

"Because I'm going to make love to you while it plays." He turned on the CD player and adjusted the volume, just soft enough. Then turned and took her into his arms, holding her, kissing her lips, her neck. He loved the way she tasted. They swayed to the music, not moving their feet. Letting the tempo of the music set the pace of their emotions.

Mark feasted on her lips as he slipped the straps of the nightgown down her arms and let it float to the floor.

A soft moan escaped her.

His hands were warm on her bare skin. He cupped her breasts, his thumbs rubbing across her nipples with tantalizing friction. His eyes betrayed his pleasure. He took his time, moving to the music. His voice, a velvety bass, spoke softly of his love for her.

She kissed him, tightened her fingers on his buttocks, pulling him gently toward her. She knew he was ready.

Mark lowered her to the bed, teasing. He loved the way she smelled. He entered her slowly. She arched her back to receive him and he moved to the music, became one with the rhythm as he looked into her eyes. The cadence of the drums increased and he plunged deep within her over and over, faster and faster until he knew she was ready to scream. The intense wave of pleasure overcame both of them.

Every muscle in his body tightened. He waited until he could no longer feel her spasms massaging him. Then he collapsed and rolled over, pulling her toward him, to nestle in the crook of his arm while they caught their breath.

When he opened his eyes, he wasn't sure if they had caught forty winks. He whispered, "Are you hungry?

"Yes."

"Let's get something to eat." Mark put his boxers on, and handed Kristen her robe. Then felt under the bed for his slippers and put them on. He reached into the pocket of his slacks for the ring box.

They both headed to the kitchen, and worked together opening the containers then zapping them one at a time in the microwave. Mark set the ring box on top of the fried rice.

He quickly filled his plate and tried to eat while she slowly, meticulously took a little from each container, and wished he had placed the fried rice container a little closer to her.

Then she started to sit down.

"Don't forget the fried rice."

"I think I have enough on my plate for now."

"Well, it'll get cold, so you better take it now."

Finally, Kristen reached for the fried rice. "What's this?" She smiled at him.

“The guy at the restaurant wants to know if you’ll marry him. At least I think that’s what he said.”

Kristen opened the ring box and stared at the diamond. She had tears in her eyes.

Mark stepped closer to Kristen and removed the ring from the box, then got down on one knee. “Kristen, with this ring I pledge my undying love and devotion. Will you marry me?”

“Yes, yes I’ll marry you. Oh Mark, I love you. I thought you’d never ask.”

Mark slipped the ring on her finger. He held her face in his hands and kissed her. “And I love you.” He smiled. “Now eat before it gets too cold.”

“I will, but I can’t stop looking at it. Did you pick this out yourself?”

“What a funny question. Of course, I picked it out myself.”

“Carol didn’t help you?”

“Carol? Why would I ask Carol to help me?”

“Mark, this looks like the ring I was drooling over at the jewelry store when Carol and I went shopping two weeks ago.”

“You were shopping for engagement rings?”

“No,” she laughed. “Carol was buying earrings and I was doing the drooling, hoping you were going to ask me to marry you.”

“Well, if you were that anxious, you could have bought me a ring and done the asking.”

Kristen laughed and threw a chicken finger at him.

While Kristen finished eating, Mark explained, "I bought the ring the second week of August. And ever since then I've tried to take you to a romantic dinner. I almost proposed yesterday at the beach. I even had dinner reservations for last night in case the beach plans didn't work out, but even those fell through. Driving home I decided tonight was the night. And I didn't care where or how, I didn't want to wait any longer."

"It couldn't have been more romantic than right now."

"I need to know where you'd like to go for our honeymoon."

"What are the choices?"

"It's your decision, but I was thinking somewhere like Hawaii, or the Caribbean. Bermuda. Or maybe a cruise. As long as it's not Atlanta, Georgia."

"You know where I'd really like to go...?"

"Where?"

"Montana. Unless *you* want to go to exotic places?"

"Are you kidding me?"

"No, I'm absolutely serious."

"You realize if we go to Montana, Pamela will go with us on our honeymoon?"

"Mark, it goes without saying. Of course she'll come with us. I'm sure she'll want to ride Sweetie Pie."

When they finished eating, Kristen looked at Mark, "I'll clean this up in the morning, we need our rest." She had that sly little smile that told him a quickie before sleep would be just what the doctor ordered.

# Chapter Seven

"Sorry I'm late, Carol," Mark apologized to Kristen's friend and co-worker, as he handed her his coat. "It's warm for October I didn't even need this thing."

I'm sure if you could have been here on time, you would have. But I'll warn you, Kristen has taken quite a ribbing, showing up at your engagement party without you."

"I'm sorry, it couldn't be helped."

"Here she comes. I'll go hang up your coat."

"Hi, honey, how did it go?"

"It was brutal and each one is worse than the last. We're positive that it's the same two guys. They're butchers. Sadistic animals."

"No clues yet?"

"Not one, that's what's so damn frustrating. There's just nothing to go on."

"Come on, you look like you could use a drink. I'll introduce you around. And then there's a surprise for you later."

"I hate surprises. Give me a hint."

"Here's your drink. No hints."

Mark took a healthy sip and followed Kristen. "I thought this was just going to be a few close friends?"

"It started out that way, but then word got out and it grew."

"The partners aren't here with their wives, are they?"

"Dan and Monica Davies are here. The Gillis' and Bernstein's couldn't make it."

"There is a God."

"Well, well, I finally get to meet the mystery man. We were all wondering if you were a figment of her imagination."

"Darling, this is Joshua Bennett, Carol's husband."

"The architect," Mark beamed and shook Joshua's hand. "It's good to finally meet you."

"The pleasure is all mine. Although, after everything I've heard about you, I expected you to float across the room."

"Joshua," Kristen laughed, "you're not supposed to tell him."

"And where's his cape?"

"Oh, you heard about the cape? You should only know what she did to me at a conference in Atlanta."

"She told us, had us in stitches."

"Mark, don't believe anything he says."

"What's the matter, Kristen," Joshua teased, "you know every time you and Carol talk me into taking both of you to lunch, all I hear about is Mark said this, Mark said that."

"Joshua, he's going to believe you."

"And, if that's not bad enough, I get stuck with the check. Speaking of lunch, what do you say the four of us get together very soon, and Mark can pay the check?" Joshua laughed.

"I look forward to it. If I'm paying, McDonald's okay with you?"

Joshua chuckled, "You had me there for a minute."

"Come on, Mark, I better get you away from him before I'm in serious trouble. I want to introduce you to a few people."

"When do I get my surprise?"

"Very shortly."

"Is it someone from my work?"

"No, but your partner's wife is here."

"Ah, Cheryl Lewis! It can't be an easy thing for her to come to a party where she doesn't know anyone."

"She's very nice. There she is on the couch."

"Cheryl, thank you for coming. I'm sorry Dave couldn't come with you. I just left him, as a matter of fact."

"Oh, you know I'm used to going places without him. Dave said that one of you had to stay at the scene, so I guess it should be him this time. Kristen, I just hope you know what you're getting yourself into by marrying a cop. But I guess he's worth it. I'm not going to stay, I just wanted to be sure I met your fiancée."

Mark helped Cheryl on with her coat.

"I've heard so much about you, Kristen. And we're all so happy that you two got together."

"Thank you so much for coming, Cheryl. I'm sure we'll be seeing more of each other," Kristen smiled.

Cheryl turned to Mark, "Danny is swinging by to pick me up so I better get downstairs. Scott stayed with the kids. Bye for now, I'll see you at the wedding." She pulled the door closed.

"Is Danny one of their children?"

"No, Danny and Scott are officers in my unit who patrol in a cruiser. Dave must have asked Danny to drive her over here. And Scott, apparently, stayed with the kids to baby-sit so she could come. But Cheryl doesn't know that she shouldn't be telling me. I'm not supposed to know they're using the cruiser as a taxi," he laughed. "Or that Scott stayed at the house to baby-sit their kids." As Kristen and Mark started to walk away from the door, it opened.

It took Mark a few seconds for his thoughts to collide. "Gail, what are you doing..?" Mark picked his sister up and swung her around, then looked at Kristen.

Kristen smiled. "Surprise."

"Oh my God, this is wonderful. When did you get here? Where's Kirk? Where are the kids?"

"They're all home with mom and dad. They wished they could come. And they send their love. I've been downstairs in Kristen's apartment changing. I just got here this afternoon."

"Oh, this is wonderful. Kristen, was this your idea?"

Kristen was smiling ear to ear, she didn't think she had ever seen Mark so excited. "Yes, I asked Gail if she would come and help me pick out my wedding gown."

"How did you get in touch with Kristen?"

"I called you a few weeks ago and you were in the shower. Kristen answered the phone and introduced herself. We talked for a while, making our devious plans."

Mark kissed Kristen, "Thank you, darling, you can't imagine how happy you've made me."

The party guests had stopped talking and began to wonder what all the excitement was about.

"Everyone, this is Mark's sister, Gail. She just flew in from their ranch in Montana, to surprise him."

Joshua signaled the caterer to have the wait staff walk among the guests with trays of champagne flutes.

When everyone had a glass in their hand, Joshua announced, "A toast to the bride and..."

Mark's cell phone made a pinging sound signaling an urgent message. Reading the text, he said, "I'm sorry, Joshua. Could you make it a quick toast, I have to leave now."

"Well, I wrote a toast that would knock your socks off." He raised his glass, "This isn't exactly the toast I had in mind, but... Here's to the bride, may she not want sex, because the groom won't be home, he'll be out answering his text."

Everyone joined in the laughter and raised their glasses to culminate the toast, sipping their champagne.

Mark smiled and lifted his glass toward the guests. "To all of you. We could never want better friends." He feigned a sip to politely complete the toast, then kissed Kristen. "I've got to go. Can Gail stay with you tonight?"

"That was the plan, anyway." Kristen walked to the door with Mark. "We're going to do some shopping tomorrow and, as I said, pick out my wedding gown and Pamela's flower girl dress. And then we're going to buy the material to make Pamela's Thanksgiving costume for her school play."

"I forgot about that. When is it?"

"Not until a week before Thanksgiving. Don't worry, I'll remind you. Then Gail and I will go to the caterer to choose the menu and do some food tasting for the reception. You should be included in that, but you just don't have time for all this."

"Thank you for understanding."

"I know you shouldn't have taken the time away from the case tonight to come here, but you did, as brief as it was, the point is you made an appearance and I love you for that. We'll just work around you, as long as you promise to show up at the wedding, because if I have to use a stand-in at the altar, he'll be doing the honeymoon with me."

"Be sure he's tall, dark, handsome and good in bed. I don't want to be replaced by just any..."

"Get out of here," Kristen laughed. "Call us as soon as you can."

"I will, sweetheart. Carol and Joshua, thank you. My work here is done.... Up, up and away!"

***

Mark stumbled into the kitchen. "Good morning, Alice. Henry. Pilgrim. Hey, what's a pilgrim doing in my kitchen?"

"Daddy it's me, Pamela."

"Oh, I thought the pilgrims had landed. I was going to look outside for a ship." Mark poured himself a cup of coffee.

"This is my costume for the Thanksgiving play at school today. It's at exactly 11:00, just before lunch. The teacher didn't want us to have food on our teeth or jelly on our faces so she said we should have it early. Please don't be late."

"I'll be there, I promise."

"Gramps will drive me to the school this morning so he knows where it is. Then he's going to come home and drive gram there at 10:30 so she can get a seat near the front."

"Sit down, Mark. I have your breakfast ready. Pamela, your dad understands the plan, he's the one who suggested that we come last night and sleep over so we'd be here early. Please let him wake up a little so he can have his coffee and eat. You're a chatterbox this morning." Alice smiled at her granddaughter so she would know she wasn't being scolded.

"Could I just tell him not to forget his ticket? You need a ticket to get in, Daddy."

Mark laughed. "Thank you, pumpkin. I'll remember. I'll be there on time. Matter of fact, gram is going to save me a seat up front."

"Is Kristen going to be there? I gave her a ticket already. She asked for three more tickets, but I didn't have enough." Pamela looked worried.

"Kristen will be there. She's bringing her mother and father and a photographer so we can send pictures to Grammy and Grampa Winslow in Montana, and for Sweetie Pie to see."

Pamela wiggled in her chair. She covered her mouth and giggled. "Sweetie Pie won't know me in my costume."

"Of course she will," Mark laughed. "Sweetie pie would know you anywhere."

"Did Kristen's parents come all the way from Virginia just to see the play?"

"No, Henry, they're here for the play and staying for Thanksgiving. Senator and Mrs Miller have invited all of us to join them for Thanksgiving dinner."

"Oh, that will be lovely, you'll have a wonderful time."

"Alice, you and Henry are invited."

"Oh, my goodness. I didn't know that. I thought we'd be having dinner here."

"It's at their apartment in Manhattan where Kristen lives."

"Mark, I wish you had told us. We didn't bring anything fancy to wear."

"It's casual, Alice. Very casual."

"Gram, wait until you see Kristen's house, it has a man that opens the door, and elevators, and..."

"It's an apartment in a high-rise on Park Avenue. Across the street from Central Park. The dinner will be catered. And Alice, you will really like the Senator and Mrs Miller. I shouldn't keep referring to them as Senator and Mrs, their names are Edward and Marlene. They're just regular folks like us. Matter of fact, Marlene is just learning how to quilt and is looking forward to getting a few pointers from you. I told her about your quilt rack and now she wants one."

"Oh my, I'm looking forward to meeting her."

"And Henry, Ed wants to discuss your experiences with the Veteran's Administration, good, bad or indifferent. He's on a committee and he feels it would be helpful to have some inside information, as he calls it. I told him you had been in the Submarine Service when you were in the navy and he wants to know all about that."

"So they are just regular folks?"

"Yes. Down to earth."

"Well, young lady, it's getting to be that hour." Henry drank the last of his coffee. "Let's get going so you're not late for school."

"Daddy, remember you can't wave to me when I'm on the stage."

"Want to make a bet, Pilgrim?" Mark laughed, and kissed her cheek.

"Grampa, tell him. He always waves and he's not supposed to."

"Your father does what he wants and if he wants to wave to you on the stage, then that's what he's going to do. And I'm going to wave to you on the stage if you don't get in that car."

"Gram, you've got to do something about them."

When Pamela was out of earshot, Alice looked at Mark, "She is her mother's daughter."

"I'm glad I'm not the only one to notice." Mark laughed. "She's always one step ahead of me. She twists me like a pretzel with her logic, just like Jessica used to do. I'm just lucky I've already had practice. And you know I mean that lovingly."

"Coming from you, I wouldn't think otherwise."

# Chapter Eight

"Captain Winslow, sorry to disturb you, but we've got a truck driver here at the station. He's turning himself in as an accessory to murder."

"Call Lieutenant Constantino and have him handle this. What the hell are you waking me up at two o'clock in the morning for?"

"The lieutenant is here, he asked that I call you. There's a problem. The driver has his tractor-trailer parked on the street in front of the station and none of the cruisers can get in or out. We've got a traffic jam and..."

"Well," Mark yelled, "tell him to move the goddamn thing."

"We would, captain, but the problem is there's a guy in the back of the trailer with a shotgun who won't get out, because he's guarding the freight. The alleged murder occurred over in the Garment District and these two guys came here and won't move the truck until they talk to you."

Mark sat up in bed and reached to turn on the lamp. "Tell the driver to move his rig to the back of the station. I'll be right there." Mark slammed the phone down then turned to Kristen. "Go back to sleep, I have to go. I'll call you later."

"What's the matter?" Kristen asked, rubbing her eyes, and watching Mark get dressed.

"Oh, not much," Mark answered, sarcastically, "just a tractor-trailer parked across the road blocking traffic in front of the station, and some jerk in the trailer with a shotgun."

"Do you want me to call Alice and see if Pamela can stay with them for one more night, or do you want me to go pick her up in the morning?"

"Give them a call. I'm sure they'll be happy to keep her if you have court this morning. Kristen, what day is this. I was in the middle of a dream and I'm a little discombobulated."

"I'll call them when I get up. If they can't keep her, I'll go pick her up. I don't have court this morning. This is Sunday, December 12$^{th}$. Call me at my place tomorrow," Kristen muttered, as she rolled over and pulled the covers over her head.

Mark had to park his car a block away from the station, the minor traffic jam preventing him from driving to his assigned spot. Swearing under his breath, he walked briskly up the steps to the station and caught a brief glimpse of a man sitting in the trailer on cardboard boxes with a shotgun across his lap. He shook his head. *Sunday morning and I'm going in the front door.* He put his handkerchief over his nose and continued into the stench of the night before.

The desk sergeant chuckled to himself when he saw Mark with his nose covered. "Captain, I knew you were coming so I sprayed the area."

Mark nodded a thank you and kept moving.

"Captain, the driver is over here."

Mark walked toward a small group of uniformed officers gathered around a man sitting in a chair. "I'm Captain Winslow. Are you the driver of that truck out front?"

"Yes, I am. And I'm glad you..."

"Move the damn thing and then we'll talk." Mark turned to Sergeant Adams. "Where's Lieutenant Constantino?"

"He's at his desk on the phone."

"Sergeant Barnes, take the driver and three uniforms with you out to the truck and have the driver park it around back. Lock the trailer doors and bring both the driver and the asshole with the shotgun in with you. I'll be in my office."

Mark was just hanging his jacket on the wood coat rack when Lieutenant Constantino entered the office.

"Captain..."

"George, couldn't you have handled this mess without waking me up. It's..."

"Now wait a minute, Mark. Let me explain what happened here before you go off halfcocked."

"This better be good."

"Oh, believe me, you're gonna love it. Hang on a second." Lieutenant Constantino opened Mark's office door, "Hey, someone brew a fresh pot of coffee and bring two cups in here. And don't grumble about it if you want me in a good mood." He shut the door. "When you came in, I was on the phone with the Midtown Precinct..."

"What the hell do they want? Wait a minute, let's start at the beginning." Mark rubbed his eyes, stared down at his desk for a minute, then wearily raised his head. "I'm a little irritated, because I'm overtired. I haven't had more than three hours sleep in the past two days."

Lieutenant Constantino opened the door in response to the knock. A well-dressed guy handed him a box with two cups of coffee and a donut on top of each cup. Then shut the door.

"Who the hell is that?"

The lieutenant opened the door, "Hey, come in here. Who are you?"

"I'm Brian Hegarty. I was sitting out there making a report when they came and got the cop I was talking to and took him outside to help move a truck. You yelled out for coffee. There's a policeman on the phone and me. Everyone else is outside, so I ran across the street to the diner."

Mark laughed, "This is a first," as he dug for his wallet. "Come in here, I want to reimburse you."

"No, that's okay."

"No, I insist, it's against the rules not to pay you."

"Oh, okay then."

Mark handed him a twenty.

"Oh, this is too much."

"It's a tip. And thank you very much. How long have you been waiting to make a report?"

"A little over two hours, but it's been entertaining out here with this truck driver and all that's going on. I haven't laughed this much in a long time."

"George, see if you can get someone to help this guy. And, again, thank you for the coffee *and* donut."

When Lieutenant Constantino returned, Mark was smiling.

"Okay, now I'm in a good mood. Let's have it."

"That's all it took to get you in a good mood? Hell, from now on if we have to call you in, I'll plant some guy out there to run for coffee." He laughed.

"You're the only SOB around here who would dare say that to me," he grinned. "Go ahead, tell me what happened."

"When you came in, I was on the phone with the Midtown Precinct. I'd rather let the driver explain his story, but the reason we had to wake you was he wouldn't move the damn truck until he spoke to you. He says he'll only trust you. They called me in when the guy in the back of the truck aimed the shotgun at them. And they weren't about to shoot him."

"What am I supposed to do now, wear a halo on my head?"

"Well, when you hear what he has to say, you'll understand why."

"George, when you're done with your coffee, see if they're back inside and bring them in here."

Lieutenant Constantino opened the door, "Hey, you two come in here."

As both men entered Mark's office, the driver, a man of approximately forty-five, short and powerfully built, nervously twisted his hat in his hands. "Captain Winslow."

"That's right," Mark said, abruptly. "Sit down, I want you to tell me what happened, from the beginning. And also the reason you came to me."

"I'm Bud Woodside. I'm the driver of the truck. We were coming out of the Garment District when we stopped for the red light at the intersection of 9th and West 37th. Then, as happens most every other time I've stopped for this same light, three men jump out from behind the parked cars, cut the lock, open the doors of the trailer and start ripping the freight off the truck, as much as they can pull off before I start the truck moving again when the light turns green. And most times I don't wait for it to turn green. I'm not brave or stupid, so I don't get out of the cab. I let them take what they can get their hands on before I start moving again."

"And you lock the trailer doors before you leave the dock?"

"Yes, but they have cutters that will cut through any lock I've put on there."

Mark was becoming interested. "Continue."

"The company I work for has started making the drivers pay for any freight that's missing and I'm going broke, because of it.

"They can't do that, but go ahead."

"Okay. So I asked my friend, Larry," Bud indicated with his thumb to the tall, muscular dude wearing what looked like a railroad engineer's hat, "to ride in the back of the trailer until we get by that particular light. Then I planned to stop and let him get in the cab."

Mark looked at Larry. "And you rode in the back with a loaded shotgun?"

"Yeah, but I didn't know I was gonna have to use it. I thought I could just threaten whoever opened the doors and they'd back off."

"You sat in the back of a truck with a loaded shotgun and didn't think you would have to shoot it? If you thought that, then why the hell did you load it?"

"Well, I figure if I wasn't going to load it, why bring it with me. And what if they thought I was bullshittin' 'em?"

Mark looked at the driver and tried to guide him back into the story. "So now you're at the light, the trailer doors are open..."

"I'm at the light, they cut the lock and I'm in the cab of the tractor laughing to myself that these three bastards are going to get the surprise of their lives, except I hear the gun go off. Now I'm not laughing anymore. Now I'm scared shitless. I started the rig moving and then saw, in my left rearview mirror, a cruiser coming up behind us, but the cruiser just kept going, so I did too."

"Did you try to signal to the officers that you were having a problem?"

Larry, the guy riding shotgun, jumped out of his chair. "The cruiser came up behind us, the two cops inside saw the three guys on the ground, me in the back of the trailer with the gun, and they just swung out to the left of the truck and went around us."

"You mean the officers in the cruiser saw what happened and just kept going?"

"That's right," the driver added. "They pulled around us, shut their lights off and kept going."

"The blue lights in the grill?"

"No, they didn't have them on. I mean their headlights."

Mark looked at Lieutenant Constantino, then back at the two men. "And then what happened?"

"I drove the rig about half a mile down the street, pulled over and ran back to make sure Larry wasn't hurt. That's when we decided to come here to you."

"Why me? You should have gone to the closest, the Midtown station."

"Well, we figured if that cruiser drove by us, they might be on the take, you know, in on the deal, and then my ass would be fried. I know you don't recognize me, and I didn't recognize you without your Stetson, but you gave me a warning once when I used to do cross-country driving and was going through Montana, on Route 90. When you put your overheads on, I pulled into the closest truck stop, the Flying J, to get us off the highway. State Trooper Kichen came over to see if you needed any help and the two of you razzed the hell out of me about my New England accent. If you had given me that ticket I would have had an eight hundred dollar fine, lost my license and lost my job. You knew that and gave me a verbal warning. And I never forgot that. So that's why I hightailed it over here."

Mark vaguely remembered, but didn't let on, no sense bringing a friendly faction into this until he knew what was going on. "Do you know what condition the men were in when you left them in the street?"

"I don't know," Shotgun whispered, obviously shaken by the experience.

"I called Midtown," Lieutenant Constantino interrupted, "and they're sending a cruiser over to the scene to investigate. I'm waiting for them to call back and let us know if they find anything."

"As soon as you hear from them, Lieutenant, let me know immediately. In the meantime, find out where we stand legally as far as holding these two men here for their own protection. Also, find out if we have to call the FBI."

"The Feds?" The driver, Bud Woodside, jumped out of the chair. "Why would they have to know about it?"

"Because stealing freight from an inter-state carrier is a federal offense. You may not come under their jurisdiction because you're the driver, but I'm sure if they're called in on it, they'll want to ask you some questions." *It'll be a hell of a lot more than a few.*

"Oh my god," Bud muttered, as he nervously finger-combed his hair, "we should have just let them steal the freight."

"Tell me something," Mark said, "have you previously reported the other incidents to the police in the Garment District, prior to tonight?"

"Yeah, of course I did. They said they'd look into it. I mean, I thought they'd at least have stuck a cruiser there at the light. But tonight when that cruiser just drove by us... Now, do you understand why we came to you?"

"I'm beginning to get the picture," Mark said, patiently. "Have you ever seen a cruiser there before?"

"No, never." The driver was sweating.

"When the men opened the trailer doors," Mark looked at Shotgun, "did you say anything to them?"

"I told them to back off, I have a gun. And one of them pulled a gun out of his jacket pocket, a revolver, and pointed it at me."

"What? Why didn't you mention that before? That changes the whole picture."

"I... I just remembered it."

"Have any other drivers in your company had the same problem at this traffic light?"

"Only the ones who have to go in at night and they're sick of it. I'm not the only driver riding with a shotgun in the back of the rig."

"You mean there are others in your company riding around ready to shoot the first person to open the doors?"

"Not just in my company. Any driver who has to stop at that light has been talking about bringing a shotgun rider with them."

Mark rubbed his forehead, then finally said, "Lieutenant Constantino will bring you to a room where you can wait. You're not under arrest, but you are not to leave these premises. Do you understand?"

"We'll stay here, but would you mind if we have some coffee? And we should call our dispatcher so he doesn't think we broke down someplace."

"On second thought, this is going to be a long drawn out process. Go across the street to the diner and wait there. Don't leave there until an officer comes to get you. Understood?"

"Gratefully understood."

"There's a payphone on the wall out there. You won't be charged with anything...yet. But I want you to keep one thing in mind, you may think I'm fair, but if I find that you've lied, I won't hesitate to come down on both of you."

"We haven't lied," both men said in unison.

"I hope not. If you think of anything else that may be helpful, be sure to tell the lieutenant." Mark leaned back in his chair thinking to call Kristen and wake her, then looked at his watch and thought better of it.

Lieutenant Constantino returned almost immediately. "You wore a Stetson?"

"I was a sheriff."

"Oh. Where'd you fit the blue lights on your horse?"

Mark smiled. "George, don't start with me."

George laughed. "You really didn't recognize him?"

"I vaguely remember. It was a long time ago. What did you find out from Midtown?"

"The desk sergeant from Midtown said they sent a cruiser over to the scene and found two men in the street. They're alive with about eight or ten pellets in each of them, nothing serious. Apparently, they were knocked backwards, banged their heads and were unconscious. An ambulance has been called. They found a .38 revolver under one of them. They'll check that out and let us know."

"Anything else?"

"Yes. Captain Walsh from Midtown wants you to call him as soon as you can. Here's the number. It's his home phone."

"Sure, he handles it from home, I have to come in, and the damn thing happened in *his* area." Mark swore again as he dialed the number.

"Walsh here."

"Captain Walsh, this is Captain Winslow. Are you aware of what's happened?"

"Yes, Captain Winslow, I am. We're checking into it. From what I understand there wasn't a cruiser scheduled for patrol in that vicinity during the time of the incident. We've had cars at that intersection, but nothing happens. Whoever it is knows when we're going to be there. We've had reports that there's a vehicle that looks like a squad car. We ran the numbers other truck drivers have given us, but they don't match any legitimate series."

Mark felt a little relieved that Captain Walsh was cognizant of the situation. "We honestly don't know where we stand legally by having the driver and his pal here. We're checking to see if we should contact the FBI, where they're hauling for an interstate carrier."

"Captain Winslow, I can't see any reason to hold the two men, but let me get to the station and I'll call you back. INS has cleared our officers. Now we were in the process of investigating people in the shipping departments and setting up covert surveillance at the intersection.

Mark hung up the phone and leaned back in his padded desk chair — the only plush piece of furniture in his office — and twisted the lever on the side to recline the back of the chair almost parallel to the floor. Grateful to Kristen for this perfect choice of an engagement gift, he fell sound asleep.

Two hours later the phone aggravated him awake. Mark sat up and twisted the lever, snapping the back of the chair to attention as he answered the phone. "Captain Winslow here."

"This is Captain Walsh."

"Did you find anything out yet?"

"Nothing more than I already told you. If you'll agree, we'll handle this from here. No one was killed. You can let the driver and his buddy go."

"Sounds good to me. Quite frankly, I don't need any more pressure on me than I already have."

"Captain Winslow?"

"What?"

"I owe you one."

Mark laughed, "You can buy me lunch sometime." Mark knew he would never see or hear from him again.

# Chapter Nine

"Skiing in the White Mountains in New Hampshire? Are you crazy, Kristen? It's been... I'd hate to tell you how many years it's been since I went skiing. I'm forty-two years old. That's past my prime."

"Oh, come on, Mark. It's just for a weekend, New Year's Eve weekend so it will give us three days. Joshua and Carol really want us to go. They have a beautiful rustic lodge that he designed. There are six bedrooms and a loft overlooking the living room. It has all the comforts of home. And it's nothing less than romantic. They even use oil lamps instead of electric lights."

"You mean there's no electricity?"

"There's electricity, but it's more romantic without it. And there's a huge stone fireplace where we can pop popcorn."

"I don't like popcorn."

"Yes, you do."

"Not for this argument, I don't."

"Well, we can toast marshmallows."

"It seems to me that you know quite a bit about this *romantic* rustic lodge. Who did you go there with?"

"Do I detect a bit of jealousy?

"No, I'm just giving you a hard time."

"You're hopeless," Kristen laughed. "All right, I'll tell you the truth. Last winter a group of girls from the office went there."

Mark stared at her with one of his '*yeah, right*' looks.

"You do believe me, don't you?"

"No," Mark grinned.

"All right, you want the truth, you'll get it. Robert Redford took me there."

Mark burst out laughing. "Counselor, you lie like you're getting paid for it."

Kristen reached down and pulled the hair on his leg.

"That reminds me," Mark said, pretending to grimace in pain, "what if I break my leg skiing?"

"Mark you could break your leg anywhere."

"What if we get snowed in?"

Kristen had exhausted all of her arguments and decided on another tactic. She leaned back in the tub they were sitting in and submerged herself neck deep in the water. Looking dreamily at one of the candles casting a romantic glow to the tub area, she softly said, "Oh, wouldn't it be romantic being snowed in for heaven only knows how long. There we'd be, sitting on the couch in front of the fireplace, scantily clothed. First I'd nibble on your earlobe and then on the little spot on your neck that turns you on. Then I'd move down slowly and tickle around your navel with my tongue."

Kristen quickly glanced out of the corner of her eye to see if Mark was involved with her romantic fantasy. His eyes looked glassy so she slowly stretched her leg up and out of the water, then lowered it, placing her foot on his abdomen. Tickling gently with her toes, she whispered, "I'd run my fingers through your hair while you returned my kisses. You would kiss my neck and my breasts..." Kristen lowered her foot slightly and knew Mark was definitely hooked on her story.

"We'd remove the few pieces of clothing we still had on, then I'd move from the couch onto the bear-skin rug in front of the fireplace. I'd reach my arms up to you, invitingly...and you couldn't do a damn thing about it, because you'd be on the couch with an eighty pound cast on your broken leg."

The spell was broken for Mark, but he didn't turn his head. A small, sadistic grin formed on his lips. He stared at her through squinted eyes for what seemed an eternity to Kristen.

Not sure if he was angry or just teasing, she smiled innocently and pulled her hands up out of the water as if to defend herself. "Stop it, you're scaring me."

Without changing his facial expression, he reached out and placed his hands on her shoulders.

"I should dunk you under the water."

Instead, he kissed her. "You little tease, you really had me going there for a minute." He held Kristen close to him and whispered in her ear, "All right, darling, I'll go to the lodge if it means that much to you."

"You will?" she smiled.

"On one condition."

"What's that?"

"That you do all the things you just said you'd do, only I won't have a cast on my leg."

"Oh, Mark, I couldn't..."

"Why not?"

"You know I couldn't do that."

"Tell me why you couldn't."

"Well, you know you have to be the aggressor."

"No, I don't know I have to be the aggressor. You just think I do. If you can talk about the things you would do, you can do them."

"Mark, don't be ridiculous," Kristen blushed. "I could say it, because I was only teasing you, but I..."

Mark crossed his arms stubbornly across his chest, as if to say the subject is closed.

"All right." Kristen gave in. "But I can't promise."

"You have to promise, or I won't go."

"You are so spoiled. Does your mother know you act like this?"

"Hell no, she thinks I'm adorable. Okay, truthfully, she'd 'biff me side the head' is the way she refers to it." He laughed. "But she's not here right now, so go ahead, you were promising..."

"Okay, okay, I promise."

"You promise what?"

"You know."

"No, I don't know. You have to say it."

"All right. I promise to make love to you."

"Then I'll go," Mark said, victoriously. "But don't think you'll get away with making a promise now and then when we get there, that you'll be able to chicken out."

"Oh, Mark," Kristen said, demurely, "how could you think such a thing? Except that Carol and Joshua will be there. And besides that, there isn't any bear-skin rug in front of the fireplace." Kristen splashed water at him.

Mark loomed up out of the water, picked Kristen up out of the tub and stood her on the bath mat. Placing a towel over her shoulders he smiled, "Let me put it this way, you will keep your promise or on Saturday night I'll make love to you..." Mark turned Kristen around to dry her back. "And in the middle of making love, when you're turned on to that point you get to when a team of wild horses couldn't stop you..." Mark nibbled at the back of her neck, then gently turned her around to face him and knew she was lost in her private thoughts — she was smiling and blushing at the same time — "I will kiss your breasts like this... Then I'll pick you up and carry you outside, drop you bare assed in the snow and continue making love to you — with you between me and the snow." Mark smiled victoriously.

Kristen blinked. "You...you wouldn't dare."

Mark kissed her, then cradled her in his arms and carried her into the bedroom. "Oh yes," he whispered, "I would." His soft lips nibbled at her mouth, teasing at first, then opened his lips, guiding her mouth open. He joined his tongue with hers, darting, touching, dancing. His fingers held her face gently then slowly moved to intertwine in her hair, pulling her to him.

He tossed the towel aside and their bodies met. Kristen's hands gently massaged his skin, loving the way the hair on his chest felt in her fingers. She slowly and lightly moved her hands to his side, then to his back then down to his white firm butt and pulled him to her. She could feel his erection eager to enter.

Nibbling one soft breast, he held the other in his hand teasing the small hard bud with his fingers, then lowered her to the bed. She circled him with her hand to guide him and he entered her slowly, teasing, pulling out slowly while watching her face. Kristen's eyes snapped open and she saw his sly grin. She grabbed at him and pulled him into her, then folded her legs around him, grinned and arched her back.

Kristen could feel his tremors as her body sheathed his erection like a glove. He tried to hold back until she whispered, Now, Mark. And he thrust into her, pounding faster and faster, both of them climbing, moaning, spiraling, gasping their way to the point where there's no sight, no sound, no control.

Mark waited until he felt her last spasm then collapsed beside her, pulling her to him, holding her in the curve of his arm while their chests heaved then slowly became tranquil.

***

"Trust me, Mark," Joshua said, as he added a log to the fire, "you'll have a great time. Have we done anything yet that you haven't enjoyed?"

"Let's see," Carol assisted, using her fingers to designate days, "Saturday we went skiing. Saturday night we sat in front of the fireplace, because we had that big snowstorm. We got tipsy and went to bed early."

"That reminds me," Joshua interrupted. "After we went to bed did you two hear the back door slam? I meant to ask the next day and forgot."

"That was Kristen and me," Mark laughed.

"Oh, did you two go out?" Joshua asked, surprised.

"No, but Kristen almost did." Mark laughed and looked at Kristen.

"If you say one more word." Kristen pointed her finger at Mark.

"Oh, did you two have a fight?" Joshua asked, even more surprised.

"No, not a fight," Mark laughed. "Kristen had made a promise and wasn't going to keep it. And I had promised to throw her in the snow if she didn't."

"Mark, be quiet," Kristen laughed. "Not one more word." She jumped up, sat on his lap and placed her hand over his mouth.

"Bare-assed," he mumbled loudly through her fingers.

"Did you say bare-assed?" Joshua laughed.

Mark nodded his head.

Kristen pressed her hand against his mouth and whispered in his ear, "If you say one more word about it, you're shut off until the wedding." She removed her hand, almost daring him to continue.

"Well," Joshua persisted, "what happened?"

"I can't say another word," Mark laughed, "on the grounds it may tend to eliminate something until the wedding."

"Will you tell me later?"

"No, he will not," Carol said. "Where were we? On yes, we were telling Mark about the cookout. Sunday we slept late, because we were all hung over..."

"We weren't hung over. Kristen and I were busy."

Joshua looked at Mark, "You lucky dog."

Carol ignored them. "What did we do Sunday afternoon?"

"We had the snowman building contest," Mark answered, "girls against the guys. And Joshua and I won that, and we're still waiting for our prize."

"Your prize?" Kristen laughed. "If you think Carol and I are going to serve breakfast in bed to both of you for that thing you made... I mean, it wasn't even a snowman. We should have known you two would have to add big boobs and call it a snowwoman."

"I don't know any woman," Carol laughed, "who has boobs the size of watermelons."

"Yes," Joshua said, "I remember a girl I went out..."

"You're a dreamer." Carol laughed, "You wouldn't know what to do with them."

"Oh really? That's what you think. I shaped them from memory, didn't I Mark?"

"And a fine job you did, too."

"We won," Carol stated, "and we want breakfast in bed tomorrow. Right, Kristen?"

"Absolutely. Anyone who performs trans-gender operations on snowmen deserves to cook breakfast."

"And since you're the one who did it, Joshua, you should get up early and cook for everyone."

"Wait a minute," Joshua protested. "Mark wanted to put the nipples on them so he has to help cook."

Kristen stared at Mark and laughed. "I don't believe you would think of such a thing."

"Yes, it reminded me of the other night when..."

Kristen gave him '*the look*'.

"Okay, I was having fun, it was like being ten years old again. If Joshua agrees, we'll cook breakfast tomorrow and serve it in bed, if you two will do the dishes. And I'll agree to go on this cookout in the snow without any further argument."

"Forget it!" Carol said.

Kristen looked at Carol in disbelief. "What do you mean, forget it? We get the chance to have breakfast in bed and..."

"Because I've seen the way Joshua cooks. He uses every pan, dish and utensil in the kitchen. Then you need a jackhammer to clean the stove afterwards. You and I would be doing dishes all day while these two were out having fun."

"Come to think of it, Mark cooks the same way."

Mark burst out laughing. "We won another one."

"After the cookout, Kristen and I will take a nap while you two clear the ice off," Carol stated, bursting their bubble. "Then we can go skating tomorrow night."

"Clear the ice?" Mark asked in disbelief. "The snow must be four feet deep. We couldn't shovel... I thought we came here to go skiing. We've only done that once."

"Don't worry, Mark, you don't have to shovel. I have a small tractor with a plow on it. I can clear a nice size skating area. We'll bring the portable CD player so we can have music."

"I'll pack a basket with wine and hot dogs, marshmallows, hot chocolate. And wine."

"Carol, you already said wine."

"Lots of wine. Tomorrow is our last day here and when we get back home we all have to be so damned straight-laced that I like to get all the drinking in that I can while we're here."

"You sound like a lush," Joshua teased.

"Oh, you know what I mean. Up here if we want to get tipsy, who the hell will see us? And all we have to do is stumble back to the lodge."

"Tell me more about this cookout in the snow. I've never heard of a winter cookout."

"Mark, what the hell did you people do in Montana, for fun?"

"We didn't sit around and have cookouts in the snow, that's for damn sure. Let me tell you a funny story about snowmobiling. One winter, it was Christmastime, so we had a lot of company. We decided to take them snowmobiling. The ranch is near the reservoir and the ice freezes so thick they drive cars on it. Since most of the guests had never been snowmobiling, we thought we'd take them on the reservoir because it's flat and covered with snow. The ranch hands and guys drove the snowmobiles over there. And the gals went by car and horse and wagon. Anyway, we're talking and giving instructions to the ones who had never been on a snowmobile. One gal said she's not snowmobiling on a frozen lake.

So we told her it was a field of grass where horses grazed. We're snowmobiling and this gal stops and wants to know what those people are doing sitting around the holes. Someone tells her they're ice fishing. She comes unglued, screams, gets all upset that she's snowmobiling on a lake. So one of the ranch hands said, 'Oh, you mean those guys near the cars and the little sheds? They're digging for worms.'"

Joshua almost fell on the floor laughing.

Carol and Kristen sat there wondering what was so funny.

Mark explained, "The men were ice fishing, not digging for worms."

They still didn't get it.

Joshua finally stopped laughing and explained the next day's activities. "It's great fun. We each take a snowmobile and I tow a dogsled containing the food and lots of wine. We build a fire and roast hot dogs and marshmallows."

"How many snowmobiles do you have?"

"There are seven here, but I don't own all of them. Friends who use the lodge leave their toys here year-round. That's why there are enough skates and skis for everyone. I hope I didn't give the impression that we owned all this stuff."

"No, you didn't, but it certainly looked that way," Mark chuckled.

"After we eat, we'll go tobogganing. Mark and I can make two trails down the hill. We'll leave one snowmobile at the bottom so we don't have to walk back up..."

"One snowmobile isn't big enough for four people."

"No, you and I will ride on the snowmobile and tow the girls up on the toboggan."

"This sounds like fun," Mark said. "We can have a toboggan race, girls against the guys."

"Hold it right there," Carol laughed. "We're not having a race, because you two will cheat."

"How could we cheat?" Joshua asked, innocently.

"Oh, you'd find a way," Kristen insisted. She looked at her watch. "I'm going to hit the sack, I'm exhausted. This fresh air really does me in."

"Before you go upstairs, I want to know about the rumor that's going around the office about a picnic you and Mark had in your office."

"It's not just a rumor, Carol, it's the truth. Mark sailed into the office, told my secretary to hold all calls, that he had something very important to discuss with me. He came into my office carrying a large picnic basket, locked the door, pulled a bottle of wine and two wine glasses out of the basket. Then, with his arm he swept everything off my desk onto the floor. Pulled out a small blanket, spread it onto the desk and said, "We're having a picnic."

He had told me a few months ago that having a picnic with wine means there will be sex involved. No wine, no sex. Then he pulled out a very nice picnic lunch that he had a chef at a restaurant make for him. We ate, had wine, sex on the desk and he left."

Joshua pretended to be writing notes in his hand, "Picnic basket, wine, blanket, desk. Got it."

"Don't even think about it," Carol said, emphatically.

"Okay, maybe my secretary..."

"Alright, just call before you show up. Will you two hurry up and get married and end all this romantic crap?"

Mark laughed. "Actually, I was making up for a night I couldn't..."

"Are you coming, Mark?"

"I'm right behind you. Joshua, do you want any help with the oil lamps and locking up?"

"No thanks. Carol and I are going to stay up for a while and talk about picnic lunches."

They always gave the guests a few minutes to comfortably make the many trips between the bedroom and bathroom and to get settled into bed before they went upstairs.

***

Mark was sitting in his office tapping his fingers on the desk, waiting for the suspect to be brought to Interrogation Room Three. *I'll call Kristen and see what she's doing.*

Kristen's cell phone announced, MARK.

"Hi sweetheart."

"I was thinking about you and wondered what you were doing."

"I just loaded my new slow cooker. I think I'm making chicken with rice soup, but you can bet your last dollar *it ain't gonna* be soup. It's my sixth try. Most of the time it ends up a very bland chicken with rice, so I sprinkle it with shredded cheddar, zap it twenty seconds in the microwave and voila, it's lunch and dinner for a few days. Luckily, I can eat the same thing day in and day out until I get another bright idea."

Mark laughed, thinking, *We're definitely hiring a cook when we get married.*

"Just so you know I'm a terrible cook."

*I know, I know. I could have used a jackhammer to get through the bark on the meatloaf the other night.*

"I cannot fathom how women figure out what to cook for dinner three hundred and sixty-five days in a row."

*Oh, definitely hiring a cook. Maybe I should start looking now.*

Would you and Pamela like to come to dinner tonight?"

"I can't, sweetheart, I have a meeting at five o'clock."

"Oh, I wish they'd stop planning these meetings at dinnertime."

"I do, too. Darling, I have to go, I'm just about to browbeat a suspect. Love you."

"Love you more."

Mark hung up the phone and chuckled to himself, wondering when she was going to get suspicious about all the supposed dinnertime meetings. *Maybe I'll suggest cooking lessons.*

His office door opened. "Captain, they're ready for you."

Mark was in the middle of interrogation when his phone pinged with a text. He looked to see if it was important.

IT'S SOUP. IT'S REALLY SOUP. I DID IT!!!!

Mark started to smile, taking him out of his terrorizing mode. He had to leave the room for a minute to collect himself.

# Chapter Ten

Mark started the car, "Your place or mine?"

Kristen thought a few seconds. "My place. I left chicken breasts in the sink to defrost and I have to get them back into the refrigerator before they spoil."

Mark pulled out into traffic and then turned left toward the high-rise apartment building.

"I really enjoyed dinner tonight, just the two of us, even if it was a little late."

Mark agreed. "It has been hectic with all the pre-wedding planning."

"And isn't it nice that your phone hasn't sounded off all evening?"

He reached over to take Kristen's hand. "Did I tell you the confirmation came yesterday for our Montana honeymoon?" He continued to watch traffic as he kissed the back of Kristen's hand.

"I wish the wedding was going to be tomorrow instead of next month."

"Anxious to get that ball and chain around my ankle?"

Kristen laughed and gave him a love tap on his leg with her gray leather-evening bag.

"I can't believe it, brutality before we even tie the knot. I better think this over for a year or so..."

"You wouldn't get away with it now that Pamela has her long, pretty flower girl dress."

"I know. She's so excited about that dress, you'd think she was the bride."

"She was so cute at the bridal shop. They brought out a few dresses, she didn't like any of them. Then I saw her looking at the price tags on the next few dresses they brought out and not even looking *at* the dresses. I told them to cut the price tags off and bring out the same dresses. Then she couldn't decide which one she loved better."

"She's probably been shopping with me too many times. Damn, it's snowing."

"Well, they say if March comes in like a lamb, it goes out like a lion. We might get a few flurries, but it probably won't amount to much, not this late in March. Do you realize we've known each other for seven months? It seems like forever."

"Actually, it did cross my mind the other night." Mark turned left onto Park Avenue. I was going to call and wake you to see if you'd be your jolly self, even at three o'clock in the morning."

"I probably would have bitten your head off."

"Seriously, for an old buck, I've got it bad."

"What bad?"

"Love. Sometimes when I'm away from you I just want to call to hear your voice."

"Mark, that's the nicest thing you could have said to me." She kissed his cheek. "I was wondering where we should live after we're married. We could live at your house. Or we could live at the apartment."

"If we live at the house you'll have your white picket fence."

"I was hoping you'd say that. And Pamela would probably be more comfortable, too. Even though she likes the idea of the door attendant and the elevators.

Mark stopped the car at the garage entrance and handed the security phone to Kristen.

In the elevator, Mark pulled Kristen to him. "Our schedules have been so hectic. It seems every time we manage to get together, I get called away. Like the other night with the tractor-trailer incident."

"That was the night you were too tired to do anything."

"I took my frustrations out on Lieutenant Constantino. And I think your secretary is getting tired of me calling to cancel our dates."

"She did mention that I'd probably be spending my honeymoon alone. I hope you'll be able to drag yourself away from work, even if you haven't caught those rapists."

"It will be a tough choice, but I'll be with you." He smiled. "I have my key out, I'll get the door."

"I don't mean to nag, but I am worried about it."

"Sweetheart, I'm doing the best I can. Did you lock this door when you left to meet me tonight?"

"I'm sure I did."

"Well, it's unlocked. You wait here. I'll just have a quick look around." Mark reached under his suit coat, unsnapped the strap on the holster, removed his SIG Sauer 9mm and moved cautiously toward the bedroom.

"Mark, nothing even looks disturbed."

"I wish you'd get that closet light fixed," Mark commented, as he passed through the hall into the dining room.

"Come have a nightcap with me. I probably just left the door unlocked," Kristen said, impatiently. "If anyone had come in something would be out of place."

"With all the things happening lately," Mark poked his head out of the kitchen, "I'd rather be safe than sorry."

"You're so suspicious of everything. I hope, when we're married, you don't bring your job home with you."

"I suppose I am being overly cautious. Let's have that drink. Nothing looks out of place in the other rooms. Oh, I put the chicken in the refrigerator for you. It's still a little frozen, but it should thaw overnight."

Kristen handed Mark his drink just as his phone sounded. "Hold this while I call in to see what they want this time."

Kristen gulped her drink down then set the glasses loudly on the top of the bar, almost breaking the stems.

Mark tucked his cell phone back in his pocket. I'm sorry, sweetheart, I have to go. There's been another rape."

"We never get to spend an entire evening together without that damn thing beeping."

"I'll call you tomorrow." Mark gave her a quick kiss at the door. He blamed her grumbling on wedding jitters.

Kristen closed the door, pondering whether to rinse the glasses and go to bed or watch television. She was startled by a loud knock on the door and quickly looked through the peephole. Seeing Mark, she opened it and smiled, thinking he had changed his mind about leaving.

"Lock the damn door! I had to run all the way back from the elevator because I didn't hear the bolt slide." He dashed back down the corridor to the elevator and heard the security bolt slam into place.

Walking to her bedroom, Kristen started to unbutton her blouse. *My mother said there would be days like this, but she didn't say there'd be so many.* She opened the closet door and stepped in to reach for a hanger. Suddenly, a hand reached down and grasped her firmly by the wrist. Her head jerked back and she was looking into the grinning face of a man lying on the closet shelf.

"Your stupid boyfriend didn't look up here."

Kristen stepped back, thinking to run, a scream forming in her throat, when a hand, from behind her, slammed over her mouth. Her bladder failed. Her thoughts raced wildly, as she remembered what Mark had told her about two men torturing, raping and murdering women.

*No*! She screamed in her mind, her eyes wide with terror, *not me*!

"Frank, she pissed on my shoes."

"Leo, move her out of the way so I can get down."

The one called Leo kept his hand over her mouth as he lifted her off her feet to make room so Frank could jump down from the shelf. As soon as he was standing on the floor, he pushed Leo's hand out of the way and jammed a rag into Kristen's mouth then wrapped one of her scarves around her head to hold the gag in place. He knotted it so tight that the corners of her mouth felt like they were ripping open.

Kristen screamed in her throat, eyes glaring in terror. She tried to kick him in the groin.

He grabbed her leg and laughed as he brutally twisted it. "Do that again and you won't have a leg." Without any warning he slammed the back of his hand to the side of her face. Her nose spurted blood as she fell backwards onto the bed. She tried desperately to roll over, thinking to run. A body landed on her, knocking the wind out of her. She couldn't get enough air through her nose into her lungs. The blood from her nose backwashed and choked her. She thought she was going to faint, when suddenly the weight lifted off her as one of them stepped up on the bed and kicked her side viciously several times. Gasping for air through her bloody nostrils, she tried to get control of her emotions, telling herself to remain calm. *Remain calm*? *Am I crazy*? Her thoughts raced wildly. *When did Mark say he would call? Tomorrow! Oh my God, that will be too late.*

They worked together removing her clothes.

"Leo, get the bag of tricks from under the bed. We'll tie her to the bedposts."

Leo kneeled beside the bed, tossed a pair of men's slippers out of the way, grabbed the black canvas tool bag of torture implements and placed it on the bed. He opened it and tossed a shank of rope to Frank. "Roll her on her back, Frank, and tie one leg to the bedpost, while I tie the other one."

Kristen tried to kick their hands away, but her efforts were futile. She was naked and spread-eagled on the bed. *Mark, Mark,* she screamed silently in her head. Her eyes bulging in fear and she shook her head side to side.

"Now, Miss Big Shot Attorney, how does it feel to be the prisoner?" The short guy with bushy eyebrows and a mustache flaked with food snarled at her as he knotted the rope tightly around her ankle. He smiled mockingly at her and reached down to caress her breasts. He began to knead them cruelly with his fingers. Still smiling, he raised his hands and lashed out viciously, continuously slapping her face and breasts. He didn't care where his hands landed.

Kirsten instinctively pressed her back into the mattress trying to get away from the pain.

"Oh, did that hurt? Let me kiss them and make them all better," Leo said, sardonically, as he stepped up on the bed. Standing over her with his wet shoes on each side of Kristen's body, he sat down heavily on her abdomen. Leaning forward he ran his tongue over her breasts, then bit one of her nipples, drawing blood.

Tears of pain and embarrassment were running down the sides of her face. She tried to turn her head away from him; the odor of his unwashed hair was gagging her. She closed her eyes, silently praying for Mark to return.

"Open those eyes, girlie," Leo snarled as he viciously twisted both of her breasts, or I'll yank these right off your body."

Kristen turned her head to look at the one standing beside the bed, her eyes pleading to him for mercy.

"Don't look to me for help. You tried to send us to prison, or don't you remember us? I'm Frank Vascione. And that's Leo Mankard. Oh, I see by that look you remember us." He laughed, maniacally.

Kristen stared up at him. *Don't show any sign of recognition*, she told herself. She shook her head, trying in vain to tell him that she didn't remember. But she did remember. Parts of the dossier she had read when she was preparing the case as a public defender flashed before her eyes.

> Francis Vascione, age 35, broken home, previous ward of the State, raised in foster homes. Believed to have raped a three year old girl in one of the homes. Hates his mother. Believed to have psychopathic and masochistic tendencies.

> Leonard Mankard, age 29, brain damage at birth, in and out of reform schools and mental hospitals. Easily led by others.

But that was years ago, before she got the job with Gillis, Davies & Bernstein.

She could see scratch marks on his face, with fresh blood that he kept dabbing.

*Yes, I remember you, you're the filthy pigs who raped and tortured that twelve year old girl. I knew you were guilty, you bastard. I should have castrated you myself when you jeered at me outside the court after they let you off on a technicality. Why didn't I realize? If I had put two and two together I could have told Mark and they would have been caught by now.*

"Look at those eyes, Leo. She remembers us. Don't you, bitch? You can shake your head all you want," Frank said, between clenched teeth — the few he had. "But I just saw hatred in your eyes so now I know you remember us. Give me one of those pins, Leo."

Leo quickly handed him one of the eight-inch needles and then leaned over her as he took another drag on the cigarette he had just lit. He looked at it to be sure the head was hot enough, then leered at her as he slowly crushed the cigarette into her breast.

Kristen's scream was muffled by the gag stuffed in her mouth.

"Come on, Frank, let's get started. I always wanted to fuck a lady lawyer. Especially, this one."

***

Mark stepped out of the elevator on the twenty-first floor of Kristen's building. He purposely hadn't told Kristen that he'd been called to a rape scene upstairs in the same building. He didn't want her to worry.

"In here, Captain Winslow."

*No, it can't be. This is Joshua and Carol Bennett's apartment.*

Mark followed the uniform through the open door, dreading what he would see.

"It's a mess. A couple of guys got sick when they saw it. They're out on the terrace getting some fresh air."

"It's that bad?"

"I'm afraid so. It appears to be the same MO as the others, only worse."

"Where's the body?"

"In there, sir." The uniform indicated by pointing toward the bedroom. "Caucasian, late thirties, wedding ring. Do you mind if I don't go in with you?"

"No, Doug, stay here. I'll take a look. Has CSI been here yet?

"Just got here a few minutes ago, they're working in the kitchen, waiting for the Medical Examiner before they touch anything in the bedroom."

Mark stepped to the bedroom door and stopped in his tracks. *Carol.* She was hanging upside down, by one leg, from a light fixture that was dangling from the ceiling. Her eyes, wide with fear stared straight ahead, seeing nothing. Long needles were stuck through her lips to keep her from screaming, but blood and bile now oozed through a small opening where her lips had pursed.

Mark turned and walked back into the living room, his stomach threatening to regurgitate. "Has that phone been dusted for prints?"

"Not yet."

"Use your cell phone, call the station and tell Lieutenant Constantino... No, he's on medical leave. Tell them I want Sergeant Lewis up here now. If he isn't on call, tell them to find him."

As Doug was dialing, Mark asked, "Who found the body?"

"I found her."

Mark snapped his head to look at the white velvet couch and recognized the housekeeper, Mrs Ross.

"Captain, Sergeant Lewis is on his way."

Mark whispered to Doug, "Did she see anyone?"

"No, this was her day off. She's the live-in maid." Doug checked his notepad. "Mrs Ross called us as soon as she got here and saw what had happened."

"I know who she is," Mark whispered. "If she didn't see anything, what the hell did you keep her here for, get her out of here now!"

"But Captain, I thought you'd want to question her."

"If she didn't see anything, get her out of here."

"She lives here and told me she doesn't have any place else to stay. Where will I take her?"

"Well, she can't stay here." Mark turned and pulled Mrs Ross into his arms and held her quivering body. Whispering softly to her, "You can't stay here." She was shaking so bad, Mark asked, "Do you want to go to a hospital or stay with your children?"

"Captain Winslow, I would go to my daughter's house, but I don't have enough money with me to get there." Mrs Ross wiped at her tear-filled eyes. "Tomorrow is payday, so I foolishly didn't worry about how much I spent while I was shopping. If, if you could just loan me a little change I can take the subway to her house. I'm so ashamed to ask... I even told that young man that I had no place to go, because I didn't know how I would get there." Mrs Ross began to cry. "I went downstairs to Kristen's apartment, but she wasn't home. So I came back up here and waited in the hall until the police came. And then I remembered that I didn't lock Kristen's door."

*Oh, so that's why it was unlocked.* "This officer will take you downstairs and get you a cab." Mark reached out to take Mrs Ross' hand and slipped three twenties into it.

"Captain, I can't take all this money from you."

"Okay, we'll make it a loan. You can pay me back when you have it." Mark waited until Doug escorted Mrs Ross into the hall, then walked toward the terrace, thinking, *She's a tough old broad. She watched over Kristen and Carol like a mother hen.* He opened the glass slider and felt revived by the frigid night air. "Let's go, men. The corridors are starting to fill with other tenants. Find out if any of them saw anyone. If not, send them back to their apartments. As an afterthought, "I don't want information given to anyone. I don't care how important they think they are. None!"

Mark's partner, Sergeant Dave Lewis, a powerfully built man with a barrel chest and slim waist, fastidious in appearance and a stickler for detail, entered the living room. "Oh, there you are, Mark. Doug called and said you wanted me here right away."

"Yes, I do. It's the worst I've ever seen. The woman has been bound and gagged, sexually assaulted and tortured. Her body is almost mutilated. She's in there," Mark pointed toward the bedroom, "hanging upside down by the ankle and they've filled every cavity of her body. One breast has been cut off, and there are burns and bruises. I'm waiting for the ME to get here before I touch anything."

"He came in right behind me," Sergeant Lewis said. "He should be in there now."

"As soon as he's done, I want to talk to him. Then I want this place gone over by every expert we have in the Department. I want the carpets vacuumed and every fiber analyzed. Every fact will be added to those we already have in the computer. I want results and I want them now."

"Will do!" Sergeant Lewis turned, hesitated, then asked, "Mark, are you all right, you seem a little..."

"It's more than just a little. The victim was a friend of Kristen's. They worked in the same law firm. Our engagement party was held in this apartment."

"I'll get right on it." He remembered his wife, Cheryl, had attended that party.

Mark turned to see the Chief Medical Examiner, Charles McAlpern, walking out of the bedroom. "We're all set, Mark. Can you get a couple of your men to help me get the body down out of the ropes? And you'll want one of your guys to tape that light switch near the door. The ceiling fixture they used to hang her from is holding on by the safety brace and half of that has already pulled out of the crossbeam. If that comes loose the electrical wires could cause a fire."

"I'll have someone find tape. Can you cover her up, Charlie? A couple of them turned green when they saw her."

"I don't wonder. It's the worst yet! I thought I'd seen everything in my years as medical examiner, but this is beyond comprehension. Worse than rabid animals."

Mark made a visual check of the room for a desk, then quickly searched the drawers and found a small shipping tape dispenser. *I'll tape the switch myself, then I'll know it's done right.*

He stepped aside to allow Charlie's assistants to wheel a stretcher into the bedroom. "Hold on, I'll get a couple of men to help." Mark stepped out of the bedroom door, "Doug, grab one of the guys and come in here, they'll need help getting the body down."

"Be right there."

"Charlie, after you examine her I'd appreciate a call so I know what you find, *before* you make your report. I'll be here."

"I can tell you now, she died about two hours ago. Bled to death."

"I could see that."

"No, Mark, not the body wounds. She died from rectal hemorrhage."

"How can you tell?"

"The blood seeped down through her intestines and out her mouth while she was hanging upside down. There's bile." The ME shook his head in disgust. "She didn't die quickly."

"Christ, Charlie, please get her out of here. She's a personal friend."

"I have rights, now let me in."

Mark walked towards the commotion. "What's the trouble, Sergeant?"

"This reporter wants..."

"I want in, that's what I want."

"How the hell did you get into the building?" Mark glared icily at Estelle Bergeron. A beautiful woman in her day, now thirty years beyond her youth, wearing too much make-up, which only accentuated her facial wrinkles. Her over-bleached hair detracted from what was left of her beauty.

"What the hell makes you think you have more rights than all the other reporters who are waiting *outside* the building?" Mark wondered how she got by the police at the front door. "You'll have your chance, the same time as the other reporters."

"You son of a bitch, let me in."

"You won't get in, Estelle. Sergeant, shut the goddamn door."

Estelle refused to move and was using her body as a ramrod against Sergeant Lewis. Lewis stepped forward, gently nudged the reporter off balance, then stepped backwards and slammed the door.

"Captain, you are going to need help getting the stretcher out through that mob of residents and the media downstairs."

"What I should do is let Estelle see the body. She'd be in shock for a year, then I wouldn't have to listen to her. Dave, clear the corridor. Then ask the doorman if there's a room downstairs where I can hold a press conference. If there is, announce it to the press. That will get them away from the front door so the ME can get the stretcher out of the building."

*And, hopefully, clear the front of the building for the rest of the night. It's going to take them a while to get her down and out of those ropes.*

Mark turned and walked out onto the terrace. Something was nagging at the back of his mind, but he couldn't put his finger on it. He took a few breaths of cold night air, looked around and went back into the living room.

"Mark, the doorman says there's a large office you can use."

"Good! You get the reporters in there. There's nothing to see so they don't need those big TV cameras. And call me when the corridor is clear of tenants. Tell one of your men to stand guard outside the office door to keep the reporters in there. Then bring the elevator up and hold it. By that time we should be ready to take the stretcher out."

"Will do."

Mark searched through the desk looking for a cell phone bill. Finding it, he tried to call Joshua. The voice mail answered with Joshua's voice message. I'M WORKING IN DUBAI. IF THIS IS BUSINESS, CALL MY OFFICE AND LEAVE A MESSAGE. IF IT'S PERSONAL, CALL CAROL.

*I'll call his office tomorrow and have him call me back.*

# Chapter Eleven

Kristen regained consciousness, but kept her eyes closed. She waited and listened. The apartment was silent. *Maybe they've gone. They must have thought I was dead.*

Every part of her body ached worse than the next. Her hands were numb from lack of circulation, and her ankles were rubbed raw. She could feel the warm, damp sensation of blood dripping off her heels, caused by the ropes cutting into her ankles tied to the bedposts. The pain was unbearable where they had stuck the long hot needles into her. The cigarette burns hurt as bad as where they had sunk their teeth. The pounding in her head was making it difficult for her to think.

She waited with her eyes closed. Still not hearing anything she thought, *They've gone! They've really gone! It's over and I'm still alive!"*

She turned her head slightly to look at the clock on the bedside table. *My God, only three hours since Mark left. It seemed like three days. I'll have to stay here like this until Mark comes back. Yes, he'll call tomorrow. When I don't answer he'll come over.*

A sobering thought occurred to her, *What if he calls and thinks I've gone shopping. It'll be tomorrow night before he comes here.*

Her thoughts raced wildly. *My hands! Can I lose my hands from lack of circulation?*

She was becoming hysterical. *Why doesn't Mark call? He told me tonight that sometimes he wants to call and just listen to my voice.*

A thin film of perspiration formed on her forehead. *If I can just get one hand free I can knock the receiver onto the table when it rings.*

Her mind was in total chaos. *Oh no, I have to go to the bathroom. I can't relieve myself in this bed.*

Frantically, she started to twist her hands trying to free them from the ropes. She could see fresh blood oozing from her wrists. The rope tore at her wounds where the blood had already clotted, re-opening them. She couldn't worry about that now. She was almost free. She pressed her thumb tighter to the palm of her hand and yanked.

"She's awake, Frank," came a loud voice.

Kristen froze in terror.

"There's no need to struggle," he sneered. "We're going to untie you anyway."

Frank entered the room, his large frame almost filling the doorway. "Untie her feet, Leo. I'll untie her hands. Since we're hungry, she can get us something to eat."

*A knife! I'll grab a knife when they bring me into the kitchen. I can at least cut one of them and run. I've got to take the chance.*

"Get up, slut. I'll even help you." Frank grabbed Kristen's hair and pulled her to her feet, then let go of her.

She stumbled forward, grabbing the bureau for support.

Frank grabbed her shoulders and stood her up in front of the mirror. Her arms fell limply to her sides. Kristen couldn't believe what she saw through her terror-filled eyes. Her body was covered with bite marks, cigarette burns and blood. Her eyes filled with tears and everything became a blur.

"Aren't you a pretty sight?" Frank said, as he let go of her shoulders and pushed her to the floor. "You're going to take a shower and then get us something to eat. We don't want that mess all over our food. Now crawl to the bathroom."

Kristen's hands were too numb to support her. She sprawled to the floor.

"Hurry up, bitch," Frank yelled, kicking her viciously.

Kristen had to crawl on her knees and elbows. She couldn't see where she was going. She crawled to the bathroom and felt the cold tile floor just before she was yanked to a standing position by her hair.

Leo removed the gag from her mouth and hissed his fowl breath into her face. "If you make any noise, you'll get a scalding hot shower, understand?"

"Yes," she sobbed. "But I have to go to the bathroom."

Leo laughed as he lifted the cover and pushed her down.

"Good, we'll watch."

Kristen knew they enjoyed degrading her.

Both men removed their clothing and placed Kristen into the already running water. The cold water hit her with a shock, but she kept thinking about the knife in the kitchen.

"This will wake you up," Leo said, as he soaped his hands, then tossed the soap to Frank.

Kristen kept her eyes tightly closed. She could feel both of them running their hands over her body. She used every effort to keep her balance. The soap was stinging her open wounds.

"Bend over," Frank said, as he pushed her forward. "Doesn't she look inviting? Warm up the water, Leo. I'm freezing my ass off." Frank stepped up behind her and grabbed her hips.

Kristen shrieked in pain; the scream became an agonized high pitched shrill. Her mind was whirling. She could hear a scream echoing off the tile walls of the shower cubicle.

"Shut her up!" Frank yelled at Leo.

Leo reached out and pulled Kristen's head back by the hair and stuffed a soapy face cloth in her mouth.

Kristen's knees buckled under her. *Please God, let me die*, she screamed in her mind.

"She fainted, Frank. We need more cold water."

"Just shut the hot water off," Frank screamed in a frenzy, "I'm not stopping now."

Kristen reached out blindly and grabbed the handrail as the sudden shock of cold water revived her. *Please Mark, call now,* she prayed silently. *Please call now.*

Suddenly, she fell forward as both men let go of her.

"The phone, Frank. Is that the phone ringing?"

Frank quickly shut the water off. Both men stood still, waiting for the phone to become silent. Frank grabbed Kristen's arm, forcing her to stand up. "Who would call you," he yelled, "at this time of night?"

"I...I don't know." Kristen sobbed.

"Maybe it's a wrong number," Leo suggested.

"And maybe it was her boyfriend," Frank said, sarcastically, as he twisted Kristen's arm behind her back. "If it rings again, you'll answer it, but you won't say anything to give us away." He pulled her arm higher behind her back, as if to make his point a little clearer. "Do you understand?"

"Don't let her answer it, Frank," Leo yelled. "She might say something..."

"She'll have to answer it. It might be her boyfriend and he knows she's home. If she doesn't answer, he might come back here to see what's wrong. If she says anything to him to give us away, we'll slit her throat and be gone before he gets here."

***

Sergeant Lewis entered the living room in Carol's apartment and saw Mark staring at the phone. "Anything wrong, Mark?

"I don't know. I went out on the terrace when I came back from that supposed press conference downstairs a few minutes ago and thought I could see lights on in Kristen's apartment. I called, but there's no answer. She probably fell asleep with the lights on. It's difficult really to tell which is her floor from up here. I'm probably mistaken."

"I forgot she lives in this building. If you're worried, I could take a run down there."

"Thanks for the offer, Dave, but I'm not that worried. I checked her apartment before I came up here and she did lock the door when I left. I know she wouldn't open the door unless she knew who it was."

"Okay, Mark, if you're sure."

"Yes, Dave, I am. Let's get on with this investigation. Did any of the officers come up with a witness?"

"No, not really. We have the usual do-gooders, and the doorman waiting to talk to you."

"I'll see the doorman first. What's his name?"

Sergeant Lewis opened his notebook and scanned a few pages. "His name is Elroy Williams. Early thirties, married, two children. Clean cut, well spoken. This is a second job and has been employed here for two years. He's been on duty since five o'clock this evening."

"Did he see anything suspicious?"

"He says he didn't, but I didn't have too much time to question him. He seems rather nervous to me. You have a knack for getting more out of people than I do."

Mark placed a chair on the opposite side of the desk he planned to sit at. He opened the center drawer and slid a few of the Bennett's personal effects from the top of the desk into the drawer. "Did you find out what he had for breakfast?"

"No, sir. What has that..?

Mark grinned at Sergeant Lewis. "Not a thing, it's just that without, as you say, too much time to question him, you certainly found out a hell of a lot."

"Thanks for noticing," Sergeant Lewis smiled.

"It's one of the reasons I asked to have you for a partner, Dave."

"I'll bring him in."

Mark lowered his weary body into the chair and waited for the doorman to arrive. *I'll call Kristen*, he thought, *right after I talk to this...*

A young man dressed in an impressive gray and maroon uniform with polished brass buttons decorating the high-collared jacket, interrupted his thoughts. Mark stood and shook hands with the man almost equal in height. "Elroy Williams?"

"Yes, Captain Winslow, I am."

"Please sit down." Mark indicated the chair on the opposite side of the desk. "What time did you come on duty?"

"Five o'clock."

"Is that your usual time?"

Yes, it is. I work here part-time, four nights a week. My usual tour of duty is five to midnight."

"Your tour of duty? That's a peculiar way of putting it. What do you do at your full-time job?"

"I'm a firefighter."

"Manhattan?"

"In the burbs. I'm not supposed to moonlight so I'd rather not say where."

"I don't see any reason why you have to tell me." Mark wanted to make this quick, but he knew if this guy remained nervous he might forget something important, some small detail.

"You seem nervous."

"I'm going to be held responsible for this..."

"Do you mean you think you will be implicated in this incident?" Mark became suspicious, did he know something and didn't want to say?

"I'm supposed to be on duty downstairs..."

"I thought your shift ended at midnight." Mark checked his watch.

"I'm covering for another guy. He's still out on a fire call."

"Then I'll try to be brief." Mark smiled. "Did you see or hear anything suspicious tonight?"

"No, I didn't."

"Were you on duty downstairs when the victim, Carol Bennett, came in?"

"Yes, I had just come on duty."

"What time?"

"It was exactly five past five."

"Was she with anyone?"

"No, she was alone today."

"You say that as if it's unusual for her to be alone. Is it unusual?"

"Well, she usually comes home with Kristen Miller. They're both attorneys in the same law firm, so they usually ride together in Miss Miller's car. Miss Miller parks in the parking area under this building."

"Does that mean you don't always see the people coming and going, if they use the parking area elevator, rather than the elevator in the lobby?"

"I can see that area, too. The security system in this building allows us visual contact throughout the building. Everywhere, except inside the apartments."

"We'll want to review those tapes right away, where are they kept?"

"They're not available."

"Why not?"

"That machine is broken."

"Does it have an electronic feed to another facility where the information is stored?"

"No, sir. See, this is an old building and it hasn't been retrofitted with an up-to-date security system. They just signed a contract for a new system, but it hasn't been installed yet. All the new high-rise buildings under construction over on 74$^{th}$ Street took priority. The security systems are being built-in while the construction is going on"

"And I'm told there's no security guard here."

"Just me."

"There's a senator with an apartment in this building and there's no security guard?"

"Well, he doesn't actually live in the apartment. When he comes here he provides his own security people."

"Have you ever seen me in this building?"

The doorman hesitated, turned his head to see if anyone was within hearing distance and whispered, "Yes, I have."

"I appreciate your discretion, Mr. Williams, but I assure you it isn't necessary. Miss Miller is my fiancée."

Elroy Williams shifted in the chair. "The security in this building is the best I've ever seen."

"I don't know how you can say that with broken equipment. And it isn't up-to-date. Did you see anything tonight, on the monitors, that might be of help to us?"

"No, nothing..."

"You're sure? Even something unusual, that you don't consider suspicious, something different or out of the ordinary might be worth mentioning to me now."

"No, I didn't see anything unusual. Everything was normal."

"Tell me this, when you're performing other functions like opening the door, or hailing a taxi, whatever, is anyone viewing the security monitor?"

"No, sir."

"Thank you, Mr. Williams. I appreciate your help. If you think of anything you may have forgotten to mention, even the smallest detail, please contact me." Mark stood up and extended his large hand to the doorman.

Mark was sure that this man knew something and was hiding it. *Or he probably fell asleep and doesn't want anyone to know.*

"Captain, we've dusted everything and have come up with prints this time. I'll run them with CODIS and see if we can get positive ID."

"Good work, Scott. Call me with anything new. I want those two bastards put away as soon as possible."

"Will do, Captain. I've got Bob Sherman and *what's her name* working in shifts, trying to match the prints to something on file. Up to now, we haven't had much to go on."

"Scott, you'll never change. You're a chauvinist from the word go. Her name is Susan Campbell and she's the best person you have in the Lab.

"I know that," Scott grinned, "but I won't let her know it."

Mark watched Scott walk away, then turned to Sergeant Lewis. "Dave, if there are any do-gooders left in the corridor send them in, one at a time." Mark rubbed the back of his neck. "And ask one of your men to get us some coffee. I'm sure one of them will know if there's a coffee shop open at this hour." Mark peeled off a twenty. *If this keeps up I'm going to have to start carrying more twenties.*

Sergeant Lewis stepped out into the corridor, ordered coffee and returned with an attractive, well-dressed, middle-aged woman. "Captain Winslow, this is Mrs Cooper. Her apartment is on this floor and she's the only one waiting to see you."

"I'm sorry to take up your valuable time, Captain Winslow, with something that may not be important..."

"Mrs Cooper, it is I who should apologize for keeping you waiting all this time." Mark held the back of the chair, recently vacated by Elroy Williams. "Please have a seat and let me assure you I'm very interested in anything you have to say." Mark sat behind the desk. "Now, tell me what's on your mind."

"Well, this evening when I got home I noticed one of my earrings had fallen off. They're a very expensive pair of earrings, so I went immediately down to the parking area to search my car for the earring. And that's when I saw two men, dressed in uniforms, standing near a car with the hood up."

"Were the uniforms military?"

"No, they were the type that cleaning or repair people wear. You know, all one piece."

"Do you mean coveralls?"

"Yes. Yes, that's what they're called."

"What time was this?"

"Oh, I'd say it was around five o'clock or five thirty. It had to be about that time, because I hadn't had my dinner yet. I was going out to dinner."

"Were the two men doing something suspicious?"

"No, I don't think so. I don't think that just standing there looking under the hood is anything for me to be suspicious about."

Mark wanted to yell, Then why the hell are you wasting my time telling me this?

"It was later that I became suspicious."

"Oh?"

"I went out for the evening and came home around nine o'clock. I stopped in the lobby to ask the door attendant, Elroy Williams, if he would keep his eye out for my earring. Then I came back up to my apartment."

Mark controlled himself not to yell, Lady what the hell are you trying to tell me? He remembered what his training at the Police Academy had taught him years before — give them time, they'll get it all out eventually. Mark tried to keep his voice from showing any sign of irritation. "And..?"

"The two men were in the corridor."

"You mean on this floor?" Mark asked, excitedly.

"Yes." They were walking toward the elevator as I was walking away from it. I passed them and noticed a name on the uniform, something to do with... I can't remember exactly, but I know the name I saw had me wondering."

"And what was that?" Mark asked, wanting to shake this woman.

"Well, I wondered what they were doing up here. The furnace is down in a room next to where we park our cars. That's what it was, something to do with a heating company on the insignia of their uniforms."

"Did you mention the two men to Elroy Williams?"

"No, I didn't think it was necessary. If anyone is in this building, he would know about it, so I didn't bother to mention it. I really didn't give the two men much thought until I found out about this horrible thing happening in this apartment..."

"Excuse me for one moment, Mrs Cooper."

Mark looked around the living room, made visual contact with Sergeant Lewis and walked toward him.

Sergeant Lewis stepped away from the officer he was giving instructions to. "Captain, what is it?"

"Is every exit of this building covered?"

"Yes, it was covered before I arrived."

"Then the two men may still be in this building. Send for the doorman, I want him up here now!"

Mark hurried back to the desk and sat down opposite Mrs Cooper. "Can you describe the men you saw?"

"I'll try." Sensing that the information had been very valuable, and feeling important, she wanted to be sure she portrayed what she had seen with absolute accuracy. "They both had uniforms. One man was tall and had long straggly hair that needed to be washed. The other man was a little shorter and was carrying a small black bag. He had bushy eyebrows and a very unkempt mustache that looked like it had food stuck to it."

"What color were the uniforms?"

"Blue, I think... Yes, dark blue with a white patch up here." Mrs Cooper touched just above her left breast. "The uniforms looked new, you know, not faded by several washings."

"Can you think of anything else?"

"No, I'm sorry, I can't. Except that they weren't black. The blacks get blamed for everything. These two men were white. I had passed them so quickly that I really didn't notice anything else, except that one man had scratches on his face." Mrs Cooper placed her index finger on her temple, as if she was trying to remember some other detail. "Oh, the tall man had the scratches, and they were fresh, you know, still bleeding."

"You've been a big help, Mrs Cooper. Can you tell me how tall they were?"

"They weren't as tall as you are. If you stand up I could probably make a good guess."

Mark quickly got to his feet and walked to stand beside Mrs Cooper.

She frowned in thought, "I'd say the taller of the two would come up to your chin. The other one would come to a few inches below your shoulder."

Mark thanked the woman and walked her to the door. "If you think of anything else, no matter how unimportant you feel it is, please let us know. We may need you to come to the station tomorrow to look at a few pictures. Perhaps you could identify the two men that you saw." As Mark guided the woman to the door, she was already planning what she would wear the next day for her momentous trip to the police station to identify... *Oh, I wonder if the newspapers will want to take my picture. I'll need to have my hair done and...*

The doorman, Elroy Williams, and an officer carrying coffee tried to get through the door.

"We'll be in touch, Mrs Cooper."

Elroy Williams stood back to allow the woman to pass through, then entered the living room.

"You sent for me, Captain?"

# Chapter Twelve

Kristen was on top of the dining room table on her hands and knees. A rope, tied around her naked waist, was attached to the chandelier above her.

"Frank, put the candle on her back and light it. I want candlelight while I eat this delicious chicken and rice she cooked."

"You idiot! How can you think about eating at a time like this?" Frank bellowed. "Look at my hand where that bitch cut it with the knife." Frank lifted the edge of the linen napkin that he had wrapped around his bleeding wound. "I should have killed her then."

"Just get the candleholder and stop worrying about your hand. It's not even bleeding. It's not even that big."

"Sure, it's not your hand that's cut wide open."

Kristen felt the cold base of the silver candleholder as it was placed on the small of her spine. Then heard a match strike. Searing pain made her struggle; almost pulling the chandelier out of the ceiling, as Frank placed the burning match on her back to burn out.

Frank stabbed the tines of the fork viciously into her thigh, drawing blood. "Hold still you bitch, you almost tipped the candle over."

The gag in her mouth prevented the guttural scream from escaping. She tried to hold perfectly still as both men began to eat. Every nerve in her body was tight, causing her to tremble uncontrollably. Suddenly, a drop of hot wax, then another and another pooled on her spine, burning then hardening. Kristen instinctively tried to crawl away from the pain.

"Look at her," Frank laughed, cruelly, "she's trying to get away."

"You better hold still," Leo yelled over Frank's raucous laugh, "if that candle goes out, we'll light *you* on fire."

Kristen froze in sheer terror, knowing she was at the mercy of these psychotic killers who would not hesitate to do what they said. She could see a pool of tears forming on the table below her face. She prayed silently, *please call now, Mark. If you call now they'll have to untie me and I can signal to you on the phone.* Kristen's thoughts brought her back to the incident in the kitchen. *I should have stabbed him in the heart, but he was too quick for me.*

Without warning, as a result of her weight and struggling, the chandelier fell from the ceiling, landing on top of her, knocking the wind out of her as she sprawled on the table. It toppled onto the table beside her, peppering jagged prisms of crystal over her body, the table, their food and the floor.

Frank jumped to his feet, knocking the chair over. In one swift motion of his hand, he swept Kristen off the table onto the floor, then raised his foot in raging anger, repeatedly kicking and stomping Kristen with his bare foot.

The gag over her mouth prevented her from gasping for breath. She sucked air into her lungs through her nostrils. The shattered crystal was cutting into her. She could feel the blood flowing from her back where the chandelier had gouged her skin.

"You'll pay for this," Frank screamed. He was in a frenzy, not sure whether to kill her then or let her live and punish her for the damage she had done. Cursing wildly, he reached down and grabbed her hair, trying to pull her to her knees, but the rope around her waist kept pulling the remains of the chandelier.

"Leo, cut that rope and then help me get her into the bedroom. I think she broke my goddamn toe."

Leo cut the rope then grabbed Kristen by the arm, dragging her across the floor; pieces of crystal tearing at her flesh.

Frank followed, limping, into the bedroom and reached to grab Kristen under her arms to stand her on her feet.

Kristen was dazed, she couldn't seem to hold her head up. She didn't know what hit her when Frank smashed his fist into her face. She fell back on the bed, unconscious.

Frank stood beside the bed, staring down at her. "Leo, get me some cold water."

"You want to revive her, Frank?"

"No, stupid, it's for my foot. She'll be out for a while. We'll have a drink while I soak my foot. When she wakes up we'll finish her off and get the hell out of here. It's almost dawn and those cops upstairs will be leaving soon."

"I think we should leave now. And if we're not going to leave then I want a go at her," Leo whispered, hoarsely, "one more time before we kill her."

"Stop your goddamn sniveling. There's plenty of time for that," Frank snarled, as he limped toward the kitchen. "She'll pay for this," he muttered to himself. "I'll make that bitch suffer for what she did." Frank sat at the kitchen table with his right foot in a pan of cold water, and lifted a bottle of whiskey to his lips. *It will not be a quick death. I'll cut her breasts off and mail them to her boyfriend. I'll nail her hands to the headboard and cut them off at the wrist. I hate that bitch. Look what she did to my foot and my hand. And I didn't finish eating. She got glass in the food. I'll make her sorry she was ever born.*

***

The incessant jangling of the telephone irritated Kristen enough to open her eyes just as Frank and Leo ran into the bedroom.

"Sit her up," Frank yelled, as he ripped the gag from her mouth, then tipped the bottle of whiskey to her lips forcing her to drink. The liquid burned her throat and worked to enkindle her brain.

"Answer it, but don't say anything out of the ordinary."

Leo lifted the receiver and held it up to Kristen's ear. She wanted to scream into the phone for help, but she could feel the sharp edge of the knife Leo was holding against the side of her neck. Kristen knew it would take only a split second to cut her jugular and she'd be dead.

She hesitated, then said, "Hello?"

Leo pressed the knife warningly against her throat.

"No," Kristen said into the phone, "Mark didn't stay the night, Tom, he's out on a case."

Frank stepped in front of her, intimidating with his fist.

Kristen hesitated, then said, "Yes, Tom, I'll tell him you called."

Leo hung up the phone as Frank grabbed Kristen's chin, forcing her to look up at him. "Who's Tom?"

"My fiancé's brother," she answered, despondently and started to cry.

***

"Mark didn't say anything, he didn't know if they were listening. He waited to hear the click on the other end before he replaced the receiver. The hair bristled at the back of his neck and a cold sweat formed on his face. He had never felt raw fear like this before. Turning quickly to Sergeant Lewis, he yelled, "Dave, the two maggots are downstairs in Kristen's apartment."

Sergeant Lewis spun around. "How do you know?"

"I've had this nagging feeling all night that I should call her." Mark stood up. "I've tried a couple of times, but thought she was sleeping. I tried her again, just now, and when she finally answered she called me Tom, my brother's name."

"Maybe your voices sound the same and she thought it was your brother."

"Dave, my brother, Tom, has been dead for ten years. I've only talked about him to Kristen."

The piercing blue eyes of Sergeant Lewis, which only softened for small children, now softened in his concern for Mark, but just as quickly hardened to a meanness Mark had never seen on him before. "How do you want to handle this?"

"We can't just barge in there. They'll kill her. Give me a second to work this out, but be ready to move quickly. I don't know if they'll be suspicious of the phone call."

"What floor is her apartment on?"

"The sixteenth."

To give Mark time to think, Sergeant Lewis walked into the bedroom and beckoned Detective Shaw. "Get ready to move. The two rapists who did this have the Captain's fiancée downstairs in her apartment."

Detective Shaw's eyes bulged. He turned and yelled, "Shut that vacuum off and stop everything." Lowering his voice, "The two suspects are downstairs in this building." Then he turned to Sergeant Lewis, "What does he want to do?"

"He doesn't know, he's plotting it out. But he doesn't think it would be smart to rush in there, because they'd probably kill her before we can get through the door."

"Tell him we'll be ready when he is."

Sergeant Lewis returned to the living room. Mark was seated at the desk, his head resting in his hands. Lewis knew what his partner was going through right now. The most difficult thing for any officer to handle is a crisis involving his own family or friends. Sergeant Lewis motioned to the officers who were working in the living room to cease and be silent.

"Dave, I've got it!" We'll make them think the building is on fire. There's nothing like the threat of fire in a high-rise that would scare them enough to move them out of her apartment in a hurry. Their only thought will be for their own safety."

"But if we sound the fire alarm, every tenant in the building will hear it. We'll have a panic in the corridors and those two will escape."

"We're not going to sound the alarm. Come on, Dave, we'll get the doorman. This is his part-time job, he's a firefighter. He'll know the logistics of how to smoke these bastards out. I'll tell you my plan in the elevator."

***

"Frank, do you think her boyfriend's brother will suspect anything?"

"No, stupid, her voice sounded as if she woke up to answer the phone."

"Let's finish her off and get the hell out of here. I'm, I'm getting scared."

"Oh no," Frank yelled. "She's going to pay for what she did to me."

"What are we going to do to her?"

"We're going to entertain her at the bar." Frank snarled as he pulled Kristen from the bed and threw her on the floor. "Crawl to the bar and hurry up! You're wasting my time." Frank kicked Kristen viciously with the side of his foot, being careful not to damage his other foot, the one *she* had hurt.

Kristen wasn't crawling fast enough to suit Frank, so he dragged her to the bar by her hair.

"Help me get her up on the bar and tie her hands to that fancy glass-rack up there. This thing better be attached to the ceiling better than that glass thing in the dining room."

Kristen was oblivious to what the two thugs were doing to her. In her mind, there was only one thought — *Mark didn't understand, he didn't understand or he would have been here by now.*

"Leo, get up on the bar and have your last go at her before we finish her off. I'll get the knife." Leering at her, "I'm going to use the knife you cut me with."

Kristen's eyes opened wide in terror. She had previously prayed to God to let her die. Later, she decided there wasn't a God. Now she prayed silently, *Don't let me die*. The final, deep-rooted instinct for survival instilled in every living being had taken over for Kristen. There had to be a way that Mark would save her. She began to struggle as Leo loomed over her, his sardonic grin enraged her, the sickening stench of his breath shred her last scrap of fear. Glasses began falling off the rack, landing on top of them. She had nothing to lose now; they'd kill her no matter what she did. She fought for the life of Mark's unborn child and that alone put her over the edge. She began to struggle like a madwoman.

Suddenly, Leo stopped fighting. "Frank, I smell smoke."

Frank came running out of the bedroom with his clothes on. "Leo, forget her, get dressed, we've got to get out of here."

Leo jumped down from the bar and ran to the bedroom, searching for his clothes. Smoke was pouring in through the vent in the bedroom. There wasn't time to put on his socks. He ran to the living room. "Let's get the hell out of..."

Staccato pounding on the door startled them. "They've come to get us," Leo screamed. Now the hunted, not the hunter.

Frank ran to the door and looked through the peephole. Two firefighters were standing there — one wearing a yellow oxygen cylinder on his back — the other holding an axe. Two firefighters ran behind them pulling a fire hose down the hall. The one nearest the door lifted his fist and pounded on the door, "Wake up, Miss Miller, Fire!"

"Leo, take the gag off her so she can answer or they might break the door down."

Leo hurried to pull the gag out of Kristen's mouth. "Just yell that you hear them and nothing else or you're a dead woman."

"I hear you," Kristen tried to yell, her voice trembling.

Frank waited until the two firefighters moved away from the door. "Let's go, Leo. The fire must be close to this apartment."

"What about her?" he asked, cramming the gag in her mouth. Should we finish her off?"

"We don't have time. Leave her tied there, she'll go up in flames with the building. The fire must be close, we'll use the stairs." Frank pulled the door open and looked down the hall. Two cops had just stepped from the elevator. Frank quickly stepped back, slammed the door and slid the bolt. "There's cops out there. They must have known we were in here. Get her down off that bar and we'll use her as a passport out of here."

Mark had his key ready, but the bolt was in place. He motioned to the firefighter, "Use the axe."

Leo raced to the bar, grabbed the knife and started cutting the ropes.

"Hurry up, Leo, they'll be through that door any second."

Finally, the ropes severed.

Frank yelled, "Get her out on the terrace."

The door splintered. "Hit it again," Mark shouted.

What was left of the door swung open and Mark burst into the living room followed by Sergeant Lewis and Detective Shaw. Uniforms swarmed in, guns drawn and ready.

Mark quickly surveyed the living room, saw the ropes dangling from the glass rack. He started to run toward the bedroom.

"They're on the terrace," Detective Shaw whispered.

Mark looked toward the terrace and saw Kristen naked and perched precariously on the cement railing of the terrace, held from falling to her death by the two lunatics. He was unable to see her face through her matted hair. She was trying to cover her nakedness with her arms.

"Oh my God, those bastards!" came a whispered comment of shock from one of the officers behind Mark.

"She looks like mince meat," another officer hissed.

Marks attention centered on Kristen rather than the entire rescue operation. What he saw almost made him vomit. His immediate reaction was to rush these two animals, but he knew he would never get to her in time to save her from being thrown over the edge of the terrace. These two freaks were desperate.

Sergeant Lewis made an involuntary action toward them and was stopped in his tracks.

"Come near us and we'll throw her over," Frank yelled. He jerked Kristen's body as if to stress his point of how close she was to death. "We make a deal," he snarled, "or else."

Mark lowered his weapon and whispered, "Don't make any movement toward them. They're cornered like rats and will do anything to save themselves." He could see Kristen's body covered with cigarette burns, teeth marks, bruises and blood. A gust of wind blew her matted hair aside and he could see her black and blue face, dried blood below her nose. And her eyes, pleading, begging him. Instinct told him to shoot these two bastards. *If I knew she could balance herself until I could get to her. Or if she could fall forward onto the terrace. No, I can't take the chance.*

Sergeant Lewis could feel the tension of his men growing. "Everyone lower your weapons slowly," he whispered.

"We'll deal," Mark said, loud enough to be heard on the terrace. "What do you want?" "I figured you'd see it my way," Frank yelled, his voice quaking. "We want a car..."

"Okay, you've got it..."

"Not so fast, asshole. We want a clear road all the way to the airport with a plane waiting. We'll tell the pilot where to take us."

Mark hesitated, trying rapidly to formulate a plan in his mind of how to stop them before they got to the airport. He knew one thing for sure, they weren't getting a plane. He stared at Kristen and saw her shivering violently. "You can have the plane on one condition; you let her put a robe on."

"You're in no position to deal with us. Just get the car and plane."

"No robe, no plane. It's as simple as that." Mark knew he was taking a chance in bargaining, but he knew they'd give in to almost any demand if they thought a car and plane would be waiting.

Kristen closed her eyes and waited to be pushed over the side.

"Let her have the robe, Frank," Leo pleaded. "Just get us out of here."

"All right," Frank yelled, "get her a robe, but leave it in there on the floor. Then get all those cops out of the room."

Mark turned to Sergeant Lewis. "Dave, move your men out slowly while I get the robe." He hurried to the bedroom, saw the torture items they had used on her. The ropes dangling from the bed posts. And the blood, her blood. He swallowed the bile that rose in his throat and quickly selected a heavy robe with a zipper front and a pair of slippers, then hurried back to the living room. "I have the robe," Mark said, holding the robe up and walking toward the terrace. "I'll throw it out there."

"The hell you will," Frank yelled. "You just drop it right there and clear out. I only want to hear from you when the car and plane are ready."

Mark dropped the robe and slippers on the living room carpet and looked at Kristen. Worried that they'd throw her over the edge, "You leave with the woman or don't come out at all, got that?"

"Yeah, you just get the car and plane."

Mark knew then that the most difficult thing he would ever do was walk away from Kristen and out into the corridor.

Sergeant Lewis was waiting for him. In the years of working with Captain Winslow, this was the first time he'd ever seen fear on his face. "Commissioner White is downstairs and wants to see you immediately."

"Fookin' lovely," Mark said, then turned to close what was left of the door. "This is all I need now."

Sergeant Lewis stepped closer to Mark and whispered, "Come on, Mark, I'll go downstairs with you." Although he was just a sergeant, Dave knew he'd better take control of this situation before any of the other men realized the nonplussed state that Captain Winslow was in.

When they were alone in the elevator, Mark whispered, "Dave, did you see her? And her eyes... pleading to me. I'll tell you this, Dave, if I get my hands on those two bastards they won't stand trial. I'll kill them first."

"Take it easy, Mark. She's alive and that's what counts. I'm sure she knows that you'll figure something out."

Mark covered his face with his hands.

"Don't break down now, we're almost to the lobby and you'll need all your shit together when you see the commissioner."

The elevator doors opened and there he was, "What the hell is going on here, Mark? You've got the entire police force and half the fire department here."

Mark wanted to vent his frustration by punching the commissioner in the face. He felt Sergeant Lewis nudge his arm.

"Well, Commissioner," Mark said calmly, "we have two freaks of nature up on the sixteenth floor holding my fiancée, Kristen, as hostage. So I was just a little busy..."

"Mark, I'm sorry. I was told they were in Senator Miller's apartment, but I didn't know they had Kristen."

"That's right."

"Are they the same two who have been torturing and murdering women in the area?"

"I'd say that's a definite yes," Mark said without sarcasm. "They've done things to Kristen..." His voice broke. "She's covered with blood and open wounds..."

"You saw her?"

"Yes, we just left them. The fire department lit some wood on fire and blew the smoke into the apartment through the air conditioning vents so they would think the building was on fire. The air conditioning system is off for the winter so we were able to isolate the smoke to that one area. When they opened the door to escape, they saw two of my men and slammed the door faster than we had anticipated. Now they're threatening to throw Kristen over the edge of the terrace if they don't get a car and a plane."

"A car and plane? Are they nuts! We don't bargain. Are you sure there isn't another way? I know you've always done things using common sense, rather than exactly by the book, but are you sure you're right this time? All of this seems," the commissioner indicated with a sweep of his hand, "as if you're using rather drastic methods; firefighters and apparatus, a car, a plane..."

"They only *think* they're getting a plane. I'm using the car to draw them out of the building and into the open. Mark began to doubt his own judgment. *Have I gone overboard? Was all of this really necessary? Was there, in fact, another way to have handled it that I didn't think of? Would I have done all of this if it wasn't Kristen up there? Damn right I would have.*

"Commissioner, would you have had me handle it differently if it was your wife up there?"

Commissioner White stared at him for a moment. "All right, Mark, do what you have to do. But do you want me to arrange for a plane?"

"No plane, they won't get that far." Mark's mind suddenly cleared and he began to put a plan together. "I'll place two snipers across the street from the entrance to this building. If they get beyond there, we'll give chase. They'll keep her alive at least until they get near the airport. But they're not going to get to any plane."

"If all goes well, Mark, we'll see you at the wedding." The commissioner started to turn away. "Have you contacted Senator Miller?"

"Not yet. And we've blocked the media. I'm not waiting around for the senator to show up so he can make a political statement out of this. And he doesn't know anymore than the average Joe Schmuck about orchestrating a rescue."

Mark turned to Sergeant Lewis and whispered, "He's a pain in the ass, but at least he's cooperating with this."

Dave smiled in agreement.

"Dave, we'll park Detective Shaw's car at the curb just outside this main exit. Make sure there are no weapons in it. And take the two-way radio out of it, that way if they get beyond this point they won't know what we're doing. Not knowing which escape route he has in mind, we can't place a road block yet. He'll expect road blocks on the short route to JFK so he might take the Beltway. If he does, we'll have them open the Mill Basin drawbridge. You take care of the car. I'll arrange for the snipers."

# Chapter Thirteen

Frank stepped cautiously into the living room, looked around and decided it was safe. "It's all clear, Leo, but hold her out there on the terrace until we're ready to go." Tossing the robe to Kristen, he snarled, "Put this on."

Kristen grabbed for the robe and gratefully stepped into it. Then she tried to signal to Leo that her feet were cold. Frustrated by this imbecile not being able to understand her, she reached up and tried to pull the gag from her mouth to tell him she needed the slippers.

"Keep your hands away from that gag. You touch it again and I'll tie your hands."

Kristen bent her knees just enough to let the hem of the robe drape on the cold cement floor of the terrace, and stood on the edge of the robe.

Wondering why they still wanted this gag on her mouth, she watched Frank, through the glass slider, as he rampaged around the living room. He stopped abruptly, looked out onto the terrace, then walked to the bar.

Kristen used this opportunity to look over the edge of the terrace to the street below. Miniature people were bustling about. She was sure one of them was Mark, but from this height she couldn't tell. Even so, it was still of some comfort to know that he was down there waiting to save her. She looked out of the corner of her eye to be sure Leo wasn't watching her, then looked down again. A car, which looked like a rolling Matchbox, stopped. She quickly looked away, being careful not to alert Leo to the scene below.

Two snipers, with their Remington 40 XS rifles ran across the street into Central Park and climbed separate trees.

Looking in at Frank through her matted hair, she watched as he reached up to the top shelf of the liquor cabinet where her father had placed several expensive bottles of whiskey and a treasured, very old bottle of brandy. Frank pondered a moment, as if he was a connoisseur of fine wine, an arbiter of taste and tried to read the label on the bottle of Marquis de Montesquiou 1904 Vintage Armagnac.

*You son of a bitch, if you touch that brandy, my father will have your head.* Tears ran down her face. *I don't even know if I'll ever see my parents again and I'm worrying about what my father will say about a bottle of brandy.* Through tear filled eyes she saw Frank choose a bottle of whiskey with a label that he was able to read and poured himself a full glass of the golden liquid. *I hope he chokes on it.*

Frank took a sip, looked at the glass appreciatively, and walked back to sit in the apple green velvet chair next to the phone.

Kristen didn't realize that Leo had been watching Frank until he started muttering under his breath, "I'm freezing to death out here and he sits in there drinking."

"Frank," Leo yelled into the living room, "she needs shoes."

"Tough shit!" And he raised the glass to his lips.

Leo and Kristen stood shivering on the terrace, watching Frank as he continued to drink.

"How much longer, Frank? I'm freezing."

Kristen thought about removing the gag from her mouth and working on Leo's obvious resentment. If she could talk to him, she might be able to turn Leo against Frank and somehow use it to her advantage.

"It's only been twenty minutes," Frank yelled.

The phone rang, startling Frank. He grabbed at it before it had completed the first ring. "Yeah?" he snarled into it.

"This is Captain Winslow. The car is ready at the front door." And wanting him to believe he was actually going to have a plane waiting for him, he said, "The plane is waiting at JFK airport at the first freight hangar you come to on the airport road..."

"Big fucking deal," Frank yelled. "A plane! What about a pilot, or do you think I'm stupid?"

"There's a pilot waiting inside the plane. He has instructions to fly you anywhere you want to go."

"Tell him to wait outside. And the plane better be empty. No tricks or we kill her!"

"There's an elevator waiting," Mark continued, ignoring the threats, "with the doors open at your floor, but I want to know where you plan to release the woman and the pilot."

"You'll find the pilot and your girlfriend together at the place where we land. It might be Mexico. Or it might be Cuba. I haven't decided yet. Maybe I'll call you and tell you where they can be found."

Mark had to keep himself from laughing into the phone. *This idiot thinks he can land in Cuba. At least he really believes I'm going to provide a plane.*

"They better not be injured." And realized he was talking into a dead phone.

"Let's go, Leo," Frank yelled, as he slammed the receiver down.

Leo herded Kristen into the living room. She quickly took the opportunity to shove her feet into the slippers that Mark had dropped just inside the slider.

"I'll hold her while you open the doors," Frank ordered. "When we get to the car, you open the back door for us. I'll sit in the back with her and you'll drive. Got that?"

Leo agreed readily, so relieved to be escaping with his life. He didn't stop to realize that Frank was going to use Kristen as his protective cover, leaving Leo wide open.

"Open the door and look to see if anyone is out there."

Leo poked his head through the broken door and looked to both ends of the corridor. "There's no one out here."

"Then open the damn door." Frank pushed Kristen in front of him, urging her along by prodding her with a knife. She was too weak to walk and was stumbling along; he was forced to help her. "We'll take the elevator. When we get off in the lobby, you walk to the car with no games. You try to play any games and I'll run this knife through you."

Her strength was rapidly fading to non-existent. The material from her robe was rubbing on her open wounds. She knew she should try something to hinder their escape. *I'm so tired I can't think straight. I don't know if I can walk across the sidewalk. That's it! I'll fall down when we reach the sidewalk and that will leave them both standing there.*

The elevator doors opened. Leo hesitantly stuck his head out to look around the lobby. Seeing it empty, he stepped forward.

Frank twisted Kristen's arm up behind her back with just enough pressure to force her to walk in front of him.

"The car is supposed to be parked in front of the door. Let's go!"

Leo held the exit door open for Frank and the hostage. Then ran to the car and opened the back door, as Frank had instructed him. Without losing stride, he ran around the back of the car to get to the driver's door.

Frank was holding Kristen close in front of him, using her body as a shield, twisting her arm behind her back as he ran toward the car. She thought her arm was going to separate from the shoulder. Kristen's eyes searched for Mark as she was propelled toward the car. She saw two simultaneous flashes in the trees across the street. In a split second, yet what seemed to be slow motion, she saw Leo launch into the air, slam into the car face first, or what was left of his face from the bullet that had entered the back of his head and exited through his face, taking the right cheekbone and part of the lower jaw with it. Then he slid down the car and slumped onto the pavement. At the same time, pieces of the sidewalk shattered and sprayed into the car when the bullet hit the exact spot where Frank had just been standing.

Frank forcibly shoved Kristen into the open back door of the car and dove in after her. He jumped over the seat and slid behind the steering wheel, turned the key, swatted the shift lever into Drive and stomped on the gas pedal.

Leo had fallen part way under the car when he was shot, and the rear tire drove over what remained of Leo's head.

Kristen tried to turn toward the open door from her crumpled position on the floor. She could see Mark running toward the car. The tires squealed as the car vaulted forward; the momentum slammed shut her only escape. She was momentarily pinned to the back seat by the speed of the car. Each attempt to look out the rear window was thwarted by the sideways movement of the car at every corner.

Sergeant Lewis sped to the curb and jammed on the brakes in front of Mark. Yanking the door open, Mark dove in. "Give it all she's got, Dave," as he reached for the microphone on the two-way radio. "Is this set to the assigned chase cars?"

"Yeah," Sergeant Lewis replied, as he careened around the corner.

"All cars give chase. Do not, I repeat, do not set up a road block. Hold your fire, there's a female hostage." Quickly switching to a regular channel and identifying himself to the dispatcher, "Have them ready to open the Mill Basin drawbridge on the Beltway."

Sergeant Lewis breathed a sigh, "Good, he's headed the long way around. And there's very little early morning traffic."

Kristen could hear the sirens behind her. She tried to look out the rear window, but was thrown, repeatedly, back and forth each time the car took a corner. Pressing herself into the seat, she worked the knot of the scarf that was holding the sopping wet, disgusting rag in her mouth. Finally, she loosened the knot enough to slip the scarf up over her head and spit out the rag. Fighting the gag reflex, she leaned forward to pull the scarf against Frank's eyes. Frank grabbed at the scarf and yanked it from her weakened hands, throwing it to the seat beside him.

She tried to put her hands over his eyes, but Frank reached up behind his head with one hand and grabbed Kristen's hair. He twisted her sideways and she fell on the floor.

He was blaring the horn trying to get cars to move out of his way, now realizing he should have gone the short way to the airport.

"What the hell, do you think you're out for a Sunday drive, move your ass." And he continued to blast the horn.

Almost losing control, he made the turn and could see the top of the drawbridge. "I've made it," he laughed like a lunatic as he aimed the car onto the two-mile straight stretch to the airport. "I knew those bastards couldn't catch me."

His laughter ended abruptly, and a look of shock spread over his face as he saw the drawbridge opening. He veered around the other cars that were stopped, then crashed through the warning gate. Frank jammed his foot onto the accelerator, the transmission shifted into passing gear and the car began climbing the upward slope of the partially opened bridge, then launched into the air, for what seemed an eternity. He couldn't see where the car was aimed, but knew if the span of the bridge was too wide, the car would plummet and crash into the bridge abutment at the bottom of the other side. After what seemed an eternity the car finally slammed down onto the opposite side of the bridge. Frank had the car under control by the time it reached the bottom of the incline. The splintered safety barrier flew like toothpicks onto the few cars lined up waiting for the drawbridge to complete its agonizingly slow function.

When the car had launched into the air, Kristen's body flew off the floor of the car and onto the back seat. She pulled herself up and could see the flashing blue halogen lights in the grill of the police cruiser as it sped toward them from the direction of the airport. The cruiser swerved to the right and skidded to a stop. The officer bounded from the car, pulled his gun from the holster and took careful aim at the on-coming car.

Kristen dove for the floor.

Instantly the windshield crackled into the shape of a cobweb. Frank grabbed his shoulder where the bullet had entered and almost lost control of the car. He screamed triumphantly and aimed the car at the officer.

Kristen heard a sickening thud and saw the officer as he hurled through the air.

Frank brought the car to a screeching halt, looked down at his shoulder, the dark blue jumpsuit was soaked with blood and he slumped over the steering wheel.

Kristen remained still for a moment and stared at Frank's back to see if he was breathing. When she was certain he was dead, she cautiously climbed over the back of the front seat and opened the right front door. *It's over, its finally over*, she cried silently and slid off the seat onto the ground.

As she sat crying, first tears of relief, then bitterness, she listened for sirens and wondered how long it would take Mark to get there. She hoped he was waiting on the other side of the drawbridge for it to close.

A moan startled her. She turned quickly and saw Frank's hand grabbing at her. Fear gave her adrenaline a kick-start and she jumped up and ran aimlessly away from the car. She frantically searched the desolate roadside for a place to hide.

"The cruiser! I'll drive it to the bridge." She lifted the robe so she wouldn't trip and ran, then turned to look back. She couldn't see Frank. Feeling sure he was still in the car, she jumped into the cruiser, which was still running, shifted it into Drive and looked up into the staring eyes of the dead officer. He had landed face first onto the hood. She screamed while slamming the lever into Park. Kristen knew she couldn't drive the car with him on the front of it staring at her. Frantically, she locked the doors then reached for the microphone. "Mark," she screamed, "can you hear me?" She could hear voices coming from the speaker in the dashboard, but none seemed to be answering her. "Please answer me," she cried. Then turning to look out the rear window, her thumb accidentally pressed the button on the side of the microphone. "Can anyone hear me," she cried. Still not hearing any answer, she threw the microphone on the floor and poked her head out the window to see where Frank was.

*The window, the goddamn window is open.* She was reaching for the button on the door to close the window when she heard Mark's voice, "....you Kristen. Are you all right?"

Kristen quickly grabbed for the microphone... Then heard a female voice, "This is the dispatcher. All cars switch to Channel twenty-six, two six. No traffic on this channel. "Ma'am, press the button on the side of the microphone to talk, then release it to listen."

She pressed the button. "Mark," she cried, "Mark, where are you?" She let go of the button.

"I'm on the other side of the bridge waiting for it to close. I'll be there in a minute."

She pressed the button. "A minute's too late, Mark. He's coming after me. He ran over the officer who shot him," Kristen turned to look out the rear window, "and he just stopped and picked up the officer's gun. "He's coming after me." Kristen screamed hysterically, "He's coming after me. Goodbye, Mark. I love you."

Mark knew they had taken the radio out of Detective Shaw's car so she had to be in the dead officer's cruiser. "Kristen, listen closely and do exactly as I say," Mark tried to keep his voice calm. "There's a shotgun just in front of the seat, near the floor. Pull it up hard to unsnap it from the clips that hold it, then balance it on the door through an open window." Mark was trying to give the instructions slowly and in simple terms so she would understand. "You will see a wooden thing on the underside of the barrel. Pull that back and then push it forward. There's a trigger guard, which is a small piece of metal that looks like a miniature saw blade, pull that up and put your finger on the trigger. When he gets in front of the gun, pull the trigger. If he's anywhere in front of the other end of the gun, it will hit him. Can you do that?" He waited. No response.

Sergeant Lewis asked, "Do you think she can actually bring herself to shoot him?"

"I don't know, Dave, but she's got to. It's her only chance."

"Most women can aim a gun, but they can't bring themselves to pull the trigger."

Cold realization hit Mark. "Dave, back up the car. We're not waiting for this goddamn bridge to close completely. Get a running start and we'll fly over just like he did. The span isn't as big now. We've got to get to her."

Kristen didn't wait to answer. She threw the microphone and reached down in front of the seat, felt the gun and tugged at it. She had to pull at it several times, until it finally came loose. Following Mark's instructions she slid the wood thing under the barrel and moved the little saw blade. Her entire body was trembling as she raised it up and placed the barrel through the open window. Her hands were shaking so hard she had to look at the gun to be sure her finger was on the trigger.

"Drop that gun now!" Frank snarled.

Kristen looked up into the barrel of the revolver Frank was holding. It looked like the opening of a cannon, aimed directly at her face.

Scenes of the horror that had just happened in her apartment flashed rapidly in her mind. She lowered her eyes in defeat and tried to blink away the tears that were blinding her. Silently, her lips formed the words — You Bastard — as she slowly and deliberately squeezed the trigger. The gun recoiled and clattered to the floor of the cruiser.

# Chapter Fourteen

"Pop."

"Well, this is a surprise, it's only Wednesday morning, why are you calling..."

"Pop." Mark took a deep breath. I..."

His dad waited about fifteen seconds, which seemed an eternity. "Son, are you in danger?"

Mark cleared his throat, a whispered "no" was all he could manage.

"I'm guessing something's so wrong that you're all choked up and can't speak. I'm going to ask questions and you can try to answer yes or no. Has something happened to Pamela?"

"No."

"Has something happened to Kristen?"

"Yes."

"An accident?"

Mark hesitated. "No."

"Is she alive?"

"Yes."

"Where is she?"

"Hospital."

"Are you with her now?"

"Home. Needed to hear your voice. Going to bed."

"That's probably what you need, some rest. Call me when you get up and we can talk."

"Yes. Bye Pop."

"Bye, Mark."

Mark went upstairs to bed and fell asleep from sheer exhaustion — physical and mental. When he woke up it was dark. He stumbled into the bathroom trying to figure out what day it was and how long he'd been asleep. He washed his hands, brushed his teeth and went downstairs, hanging onto the railing like a drunk, slowly descending the stairs. The kitchen light was on. He stepped cautiously to the kitchen door and saw his father sitting at the kitchen table smiling at him.

*I'm hallucinating.*

Paul wanted to stand up and hug his son, but he knew it would break down Mark's frangible defenses that he had just built by sleeping. Instead, he nodded toward the coffee pot. "There's fresh coffee. I just made it."

"Oh, it's really you. I mean when, when did you get here?"

"About half an hour ago."

Oh my god, Pop, I didn't mean for you to fly all the way out here. I'm sorry, I..."

"When my intrepid son calls me and can't talk, where else would I be? Get yourself a cup of coffee, sit down and tell me what's got your panties in a twist." His father knew this wasn't the time to treat his son with kid gloves. He had never seen his son in this much anguish. No matter what Mark had ever faced, he'd always had grit. Too much grit sometimes.

"I'll reimburse you the money for the tickets."

"I won't accept it, so get that thought right out of your head."

Mark turned to pour his coffee and smiled. He knew, 'so get that thought right out of your head' meant don't bring it up again, end of story'. It was the warning sentence when they were kids that stopped them from repeatedly asking for something. "Are you hungry, Pop?"

"A little. I could eat a couple of donuts."

"I don't have any donuts."

"Well, it just happens I brought them with me."

"Where are they?" Mark smiled. "I'm starving."

"I figured you would be by the time I got here."

"I, I can't believe you're really here. When I saw you sitting there just now, I thought you were a figment of my imagination."

His dad smiled, "I knew that when I saw the *deer in the headlights* look on your face." Paul stood up, got the box of donuts and put them on the table. He was biding his time; he knew his son would start talking when he was ready.

Mark sat down. "Remember I told you about the case I was working on?"

*Oh, dear god, no, not Kristen. No wonder he couldn't talk.* "I remember something about it." He remembered every word his son had told him about it.

"There were two of them... They... They, uh..."

*Time to talk about something else.* "Where's Pamela?"

"She's with Alice and Henry. They came and got her when they heard on the news that Kristen had been, had been..."

"That was very nice of them. They're good people. She likes staying there with them, doesn't she?"

Mark smiled. "Yes, they spoil her. She told me she likes to stay there as long as she knows that I'll always come and get her. When she told me that..."

"You had to do the old thumbnail in the palm trick?"

Mark chuckled. "Yes. How did you know that?"

"Your sister, Gail. Your mother used to tease me when she'd catch me wiping me eyes. She'd smile and say, 'Oh, my tough guy has a soft spot.' While I'm here I think I'll take a ride to see Pamela, Alice and Henry. Pamela will be upset that I didn't bring Sweetie Pie with me."

They both broke up laughing.

"Does Pamela like Kristen?"

"She adores her. They do a lot of things together. At Christmas she took Pamela to see the 'Nutcracker' and the Christmas show with the Rockettes at Radio City Music Hall.

"While I'm here I'd like to meet Kristen."

"She's in the hospital in a coma."

"So, the thing you can't tell me is the rapists got Kristen and that's why she's in the hospital?"

"Yes."

"This is what I'd like to do and in this order, see Kristen, see where you work, drive to Connecticut to see Pamela and fly home. That okay with you?"

"Of course, whatever you want to do."

"Good. After I see Pamela, I'll drive to the airport where I landed, drop off the rental and head home. I'll work at my own pace and I don't want you trying to make time to come to the airport to wave at the plane. I'm a big boy, I can get on the plane by myself."

"Okay, Pop, I get the picture." Mark knew his dad didn't want him taking time from his duties.

His dad smiled. "And we'll see you when you all come to visit. And who knows, maybe to live, if I get my wish."

"Kristen said she wanted to go there for the honeymoon, but that was before all this happened."

"Okay. The sun has come up. Why don't you get dressed, then we'll stop for breakfast and head to the hospital."

"Okay. I'll be right down. Do you need anything?"

"Not at the moment. I'm going to call your mother, she should be up by now. Let her know when I'll be home. What is it, a two hour time change?"

"Yes."

"No wonder the flight seemed longer coming this way than it shows on the ticket going back."

"What airport are you landing at?"

"Bozeman. I left my truck there."

"Pop, thank you. Thank you for knowing I needed you. Now I can get through anything."

"Come here, son. You'll never be too old to hug."

***

"Captain, I brought you some coffee," the private duty nurse said, as she placed the mug on the table next to him. "Why don't you go down to the cafeteria and get some breakfast?"

"No, I'll wait." He rubbed his eyes. "I want to be here when she wakes up."

"If she opens her eyes, I'll have you paged."

"No," Mark whispered, "I can't leave her."

"Now you listen to me," the nurse said, gently but firmly, "you have been sitting here for three days. You've only had short catnaps and you haven't had a decent meal. What good are you going to be to her when she finally wakes up? You won't have any strength. And besides that, if she sees you the way you look right now, with that three day growth of beard, you'll scare her and she'll close her eyes again."

"Do I look that bad?"

"To put it bluntly, you look like hell."

"You certainly have a way with words." Mark smiled, "Were you ever in the army?"

"No," the nurse laughed. "I never was, but if I don't get you out of here I'm going to have *two* patients on my hands. Finish your coffee and go downstairs and get some breakfast. While you're gone, I'll dig up a razor for you. When you get back you can shower and shave right here in Kristen's bathroom."

"Okay, you win." Mark finished his coffee. "I'll be back shortly."

"While you're gone I'll give Kristen a sponge bath and tend to her wounds. The doctor will be here at nine o'clock and he wants to speak to you then. And don't hurry back on my account."

"You promise to have me paged if she opens her eyes?"

"Yes, I promise. Even if her eyelids just flutter, I'll page you," she smiled. "We do know how important it is for you to be here when she finally wakes up, but we also know how important it is to have you looking at least halfway decent and awake at the same time. Now go, just go."

Reluctantly, Mark left the room. As he hurried along the corridor, he smiled. *Imagine being married to that...*

CAPTAIN WINSLOW, CAPTAIN MARK WINSLOW, DIAL 899

Mark smiled, turned and ran back to the room. As he entered he looked at Kristen, her eyes were closed. Mrs Wheeler, I was just paged. Did you..?"

"No, it wasn't me."

Mark reached for the phone on the bedside table and dialed 899. "This is Mark Winslow responding to a page."

"Yes sir, I have a call for you. I'll put it through."

"Mark, this is Joshua Bennett. I just got your message, they said you called three days ago. I tried calling your cell phone, but kept getting your voice mail, so I tried the police station. They said you're at the hospital. What's going on?"

"Joshua, are you home now?"

"No. I'm in Dubai."

Mark pulled the phone into the bathroom and closed the door so Kristen couldn't hear what he was saying. He wasn't sure if she could hear him, but he wasn't taking any chances. "Joshua, I have some very bad news. Please sit down."

"I am sitting down at my desk. What's wrong, did something happen to Kristen?"

"I called you, because Carol died."

"What?! Was she in an accident? Where is she? Jesus Christ, what happened?"

"There was an incident in the apartment and she was killed." Mark wasn't going into the horrific details over the phone. "Carol's parents flew in yesterday. Carol's at a funeral home, but they're waiting for you to..."

"Mark, can you contact them and tell them I'm on my way?"

"Yes. When you get to New York, call me no matter what time day or night and I'll send a car for you."

"Why are you at the hospital?"

"Kristen is in the hospital. I'll fill you in when you get here."

"The flight takes about thirteen hours." Joshua hung up.

`Mark wiped his eyes and made his way out of the room into the hall. Kristen's mother touched his arm. "Did Kristen wake up?"

"No, not yet. The nurse you hired is sending me down to get some breakfast."

Edward laughed, "Oh, she's a pistol."

"She's going to give Kristen a sponge bath and tend to her wounds. She doesn't think she'll wake up before I get back."

"In that case, do you mind if we join you?" Edward asked. "We came directly here from the hotel and haven't had our morning coffee."

"I'll be happy for the company," Mark said, as he turned to walk toward the elevator. "The doctor will be in at nine o'clock and wants to see us."

Marlene waited for the elevator doors to close before she asked, "How are you holding up under all of this? We could sit with Kristen in shifts, rather than you sitting up all night. Quite frankly, you look like you've been dragged through a keyhole backwards. When we left the hospital last night, you promised to get some sleep, but from the look of you, you didn't sleep a wink."

"Now, Marlene, don't start on the boy," Edward said, standing aside to allow his wife to exit the elevator.

Mark chuckled to himself, he never felt so young as when Edward was around.

Mark and Edward went to the self-service counter, and then joined Marlene moments after she was able to locate an empty table.

As they sat down, Marlene asked Mark, "Do you think you should postpone the wedding, it's only three weeks away and..."

"I don't know," Mark rubbed his forehead. "I just don't know. I keep thinking we should leave the plans as they are so we'll have something happy to talk about when Kristen comes out of this. But on the other hand..."

"On the other hand," Edward interrupted, "Will she be strong enough to handle her wedding day?"

"Perhaps we should postpone it until we're sure she's strong enough."

"And we have to think of the guests who will be coming in from out of town."

"Good point, Marlene."

"Why don't we wait to see what the doctor has to say," Marlene suggested, "before we make any changes or decisions. That way we'll have something positive to work with."

"That's an excellent idea," Mark agreed, wiping the corner of his mouth with a napkin.

"Does anyone want more coffee?"

"I could stand another cup." Marlene handed her empty mug to her husband. "How about you, Mark?"

"There's Doctor Bagley. I'll get coffee all around."

"Sit still," Edward said. "I'm up."

Mark signaled to the middle-aged, meticulously dressed man standing just inside the entrance to the cafeteria.

"Here you are," Doctor Bagley said with enthusiasm, as he walked toward the table. "I was a little early on my rounds and that sergeant you hired as a private-duty nurse told me that Mark was down here. My God, imagine being married to her?"

Mark smiled and pulled out a chair for the doctor. "Those were my exact thoughts earlier."

"She's very good with Kristen," Marlene pointed out.

"We don't dispute that, Marlene," Doctor Bagley laughed, "it's the rest of us who suffer."

"I got you a cup, too, Nathan," Edward said, returning to the table carrying a tray of steaming coffee mugs. "I'm sure you can use it at this time of the morning."

"Thanks, Edward." Doctor Bagley gingerly removed a mug from the tray and took a cautious sip. Placing the cup on the table, he stared at it for a moment. "I'm glad I found you all together, because

I have something to tell you. I've been a friend of this family for over thirty years. I've been Kristen's doctor ever since she moved here. And Edward's doctor whenever he's in town. So I'll get right to the point." He looked directly at Mark. "Kristen will never be able to have anymore children." He purposely didn't say anything about the fetus. He wasn't sure if her parents were aware that she's pregnant. Only Mark picked up on the 'anymore'. *What did he mean by anymore? Had she been pregnant before? Was she pregnant now?*

Doctor Bagley saw the look of surprise on Mark's face.

"Never?!" Marlene gasped. "Nathan, are you sure? My god, it's all she's ever dreamed of... All she's ever wished for. After Richard died she thought she would never meet anyone else and wanted to be artificially inseminated. It was that important to her." Marlene covered her face with her hands. "Why, why did I ever talk her out of it? It's all my fault," she cried, sobbing uncontrollably.

Mark turned in his chair trying desperately to blink back the tears that were welling up in his eyes. He was surprised to see the cafeteria was empty, except for the worker behind the steam table and two interns sitting, half asleep, in the far corner. He could hear Edward and Doctor Bagley trying to console Marlene.

He turned and pounded his fist on the table. "Your fault, Marlene? Don't you think you're being a little selfish?" His voice became a guttural whisper, "When, in fact, this is all my fault."

"Your fault?" Marlene raised her head to look at him. "It's not your fault, Mark."

"Yes, my fault. We've all sat upstairs in Kristen's room for three days and nights. The entire time I keep asking myself why didn't I go down to her apartment that night when I first wondered why she didn't answer her phone. I could have prevented all of this."

"Yes," Edward interrupted, "and they might have killed her while you were playing hero. You did the right thing. It's my fault, I should not have allowed her to live in Manhattan alone."

"Now wait a minute," Doctor Bagley said, firmly, realizing he should have kept his mouth shut. "The blame is with the two men who did this." He knew he had to get Mark aside and explain. "The fact remains that we have a very sick woman upstairs, physically and emotionally. And she is our main concern right now. I suggest you postpone the wedding indefinitely."

"Whether Kristen can or cannot have children is not the reason I'm marrying her. That's not the issue..."

"Calm down, Mark. The reason I suggested postponing it is I honestly don't know how she will be mentally when she comes out of this sleep she's in."

"She will wake up, won't she, Nathan?"

"Yes, Marlene, but I don't know when. Right now her subconscious is blocking out the horror she's been through. To put it in lay terms, she is not in an actual coma. She just doesn't want to wake up. She may have lost her will to live so it's important for all of you to sit and talk to her."

"What should we talk about?"

"Marlene, you talk about happy things from her childhood. Anything happy. The wedding, her friends. Just do not mention what happened. Keep talking as if she's awake. We did a brain scan on her yesterday and we're fairly sure that she can hear and understand what is said. I suggest that while you're talking, ask her questions, then give her a chance to think of an answer. Assume she's answered correctly and then continue talking. Try not to say anything to upset her. Nothing negative."

"Nothing negative?" Edward chuckled to break the mood, "In that case maybe we should get rid of that bossy nurse I hired."

Doctor Bagley smiled. "She'll be the best one to have around. She's very protective and once Kristen wakes up she'll have her up on her feet in no time. She has a degree in psychology, so she'll be a big help in getting Kristen through all of this."

"I like her, she doesn't mince words, says what she thinks *if* she thinks it's important for the wellbeing of us or Kristen. Matter of fact, she told me to shower and shave, because I look like hell."

"Well, you do, my boy, you do," Edward laughed.

CAPTAIN WINSLOW, CAPTAIN WINSLOW, DIAL 899

Mark's page came loud and clear from the speaker mounted over their heads.

Doctor Bagley pointed, "There's a phone over there on the wall."

"Maybe she's awake," Marlene said, hopefully.

"Sorry, Marlene, they would have paged me first," Doctor Bagley stated.

Marlene's eyes followed Mark as he hurried to the phone. She watched his facial expressions change as he spoke, first from expectant joy to a scowl. She turned to Doctor Bagley, "I think you're right."

"Let's wait and see," Edward said, as he took Marlene's hand into his.

Mark hurried back to the table, but didn't sit down. "That was Lieutenant Constantino from my department. We're placing guards outside Kristen's door. The psycho has struck again."

"Edward take Marlene up to Kristen's room. I want a quick word with Mark."

'All right. We'll stay with Kristen until you get there, Mark."

"I'll be right along."

Doctor Bagley waited a moment for Marlene and Ed to walk around the corner. "Mark, I take it you didn't know Kristen is pregnant?"

"Is she?"

"Yes."

Mark leaned against the wall to steady himself. "How far along?"

"We did an ultrasound, we think ten weeks."

"Do you know if it's a boy or girl?"

"Not yet, that usually takes sixteen to eighteen weeks."

"How did you know she was pregnant?"

"She called me looking for a good OB. I referred her, they set up an appointment, but when she didn't show up, their office called me. The appointment was for the morning after all this happened." "Oh. Oh?!" Mark smiled. "So she didn't know for sure and that's probably why she didn't tell me."

"I'm sure that's the reason. I know she was very excited when she called me. And, Mark, I apologize for opening my big mouth in front of Marlene and Ed. I should know better."

"Don't worry about it, Doc. Things are a bit hairy right now, so none of us are thinking correctly. I'm sorry, but I have to run. If you're going up to Kristen's room, I think you could tell her parents the good news, it will help them."

"I think I'll wait on that. I'll leave that to you and Kristen. Just give me one more minute. The baby will have to be delivered cesarean and Kristen will need reconstructive surgery afterward."

Mark stared at him. "But she will live?"

"Yes. It will be a long haul. My suggestion is cancel the wedding. Get married now. You can have a private ceremony in her room. Otherwise, you'll have to go through me for information and I'm not always available. The other doctors will not be able to tell you anything, because you're not married. I'm not trying to cause strife in the family, but you know Edward is a very strong personality and he could very well insist that she recuperate in Virginia. And then have the baby in Virginia. Are you following where I'm going here?"

Mark didn't say anything, just kept nodding his head.

"And I trust you'll keep this conversation between the two of us."

"Positively." I can't thank you enough. And I understand you're not saying it would happen, only that the possibility is there."

"Let me just say, it's more than just there, it may be a consideration in the works. I'd move things right along, if I were you. In the patient's best interest, of course."

"I have to run and set up security for her. Thank you, thank you very much for the heads up."

"Well, I think you've been through enough. You don't want to lose another... I've said enough. Now I'll go up and see how Kristen is doing."

# Chapter Fifteen

He was the captain of the ship he sat behind and he had all his ship's flags flying on his 'me wall' to prove it. Mark wondered if his kindergarten diploma was up there. The brass name plate — Ronald E. Fitzgerald - Hospital Director — sat on the desk in front of him. The haircut probably cost two hundred bucks. His dark brown eyes, behind the glasses perched on the end of his nose, clearly sent the message, don't screw with me.

Fitzgerald sat quietly, listening intently to Mark. "We think he'll come here to the hospital, because Kristen Miller is the only one who can identify and testify against him."

"But I don't understand. The newspapers reported that she shot him."

"She did, however, he had grabbed at the barrel of the shotgun with his left hand, trying to pull it away from her, just as she pulled the trigger. Two of his fingers were shot off. I arrived at the scene as it was happening."

Mark visualized the murderous look on the bastard's face when they were taking him away and he was screaming at Kristen, "I'll be back and I'll get you for this, you bitch."

Kristen had collapsed in Mark's arms. Everyone had turned to look at her, everyone except the officer who used the opportunity to knee the bastard in the groin to shut him up. Mark made a mental note to be sure the officer got at least a commendation, or better still, a promotion.

"Captain Winslow, you were saying?"

"What? Oh, I'm sorry... Doing a little wool gathering there. They took him over to City Hospital, under arrest, for medical treatment. When he was brought back to a room, he was under heavy sedation. A guard was placed outside the door. The nurse went in to check his vital signs. The guard may have thought it was safe to step into the bathroom."

"You mean the bathroom was in the same room, and he still got away?"

"He killed the nurse by cutting her jugular vein with a scalpel. The bloody scalpel was found beside her body. They don't know where he got it from; maybe he picked it up in the operating room when they brought him in to work on his hand and shoulder. After he killed the nurse, he drowned the guard in the toilet."

"Didn't anyone see him leave the hospital?"

"No. The guard was left in his underwear when they found his body, so we're sure the killer wore the guard's uniform to make his escape."

"I'll cooperate in any way possible, Captain Winslow, but I must make it very clear that my main concern is for the patients in this hospital. They must not be disturbed by any of your police work."

"I appreciate your cooperation, sir."

"What else is it you need?"

"We want to outfit our officers, male and female, in hospital scrubs so they appear to be part of the staff. The media is cooperating by announcing that the victim is ready to identify him. Unfortunately, they had already made her whereabouts known, which forces us to go with this plan. The assailant is sure to discover her location and will try to get to her. If and when he does, we'll be ready."

"How can you be so sure that he'll try to kill her?"

"Because, as far as he knows, she's the only victim who lived. With her identification, he knows he will be caught."

"If he is free now, why would he put his life in jeopardy to come here and kill her?"

"The forensic psychiatrist explained that the killer is possibly a schizophrenic or psychopathic individual. He won't reason this out in the same way you or I would. In his mind every victim must die."

"You said that as far as the rapist knows, Kristen Miller is the only victim who lived. Were there others?"

"Just one. He left her for dead, and from what they tell me, she was very nearly dead. That she survived was a miracle. I was in Atlanta at the time," Mark offered, needlessly, as if he had to make an excuse for why he was not on the case at the time. "The Bureau Chief thought I was getting emotionally involved and forced me to take a three day R&R."

There was a light tap on the door as it opened. The most beautiful woman Mark had ever seen stepped into the room. "You sent for me, sir?"

"Yes Ingrid, I did. Captain, this is Ingrid Johansson. She's in charge of our Security Department. Ingrid, this is Captain Winslow, NYPD. He'll explain his situation and tell you what he requires. You're to cooperate to the fullest extent."

Mark stood up and accepted the hand she offered. He was dumbstruck. The woman almost matched his height. Her uniform of slacks and well-filled shirt were smartly crisp. Her short blonde hair was softly curled. He noticed her shoes, belt and holster were highly polished leather.

Mark stared appreciatively into her hazel eyes and returned her sparkling white smile.

"Captain," Mr. Fitzgerald interrupted Mark's thoughts, "Ingrid is well qualified. One of her qualifications is that she attended the Police Academy."

"Why don't we go to my office," Ingrid suggested, "and you can tell me what you require."

Mark turned to shake hands and thank Mr. Fitzgerald for his cooperation, then followed Ingrid into the hall and explained the situation to her as they walked.

Once in her office, she immediately picked up the phone and called the head of housekeeping to explain the situation. "No, I don't know how many. I'll send them down to you so you can outfit them with surgery scrubs, maintenance uniforms, candy stripers, whatever you can come up with. And Bob, make sure everything fits so it looks realistic." As she replaced the phone in the cradle, she turned to Mark. "Anything else?"

"No, not at the moment," Mark smiled. I'll get back to you."

"Good, I'll wait. I'm supposed to go off duty at five o'clock, but knowing how important this is, I'll stay here all night." She handed Mark a piece of paper. "If you need me, dial that number on any one of the red phones you'll see hanging on the walls in every corridor. Be sure to wait by the phone you use, because this locater will show me where you are. Got that?"

"Got it," Mark answered, knowing he had been dismissed.

"And, Captain, I'm sorry about your fiancée. If the bastard shows up here, you'll have him on a platter."

Mark smiled and stepped into the hall.

***

Mark was standing at the nurses' station dressed in green scrubs, complete with a paper face mask hanging down around his chin and a green cap covering his hair, when Dave Lewis was wheeled out of the elevator by two orderlies. They parked him near the nurses' station and walked away.

"How are you doing, Sergeant?" Mark asked.

"Oh, I'm doing good, Doc," Dave whispered. "I'm supposed to meet Captain Winslow on this floor."

Mark leaned down, his smile hidden by the paper mask, "Dave, it's me." He made the pretense of pulling the sheet, that was covering the patient, a little closer to his chin. Actually, covering the small amount of his uniform that was showing.

"Any sign of him yet?"

"Not yet. This is the floor Kristen is on. You'll be in the corridor all the time. Nurses will wheel you back and forth with different caps on your head. You'll be placed along a wall or left here at the desk. If that bastard is hiding somewhere or walks onto this floor, we've planned this so you'll look like a different patient being brought in or out. If you need to take a break, send one of our people to Kristen's room to get me so I can cover the area. I'm sure you'll want coffee or lunch or whatever."

"Okay. Which direction is Ms. Miller's room?"

Mark indicated the direction by looking down the corridor. "She's in 903," he whispered, then turned and pretended to look at one of the patient's charts. "Most of the nurses and orderlies who will be wheeling you around are officers dressed to look like hospital staff. Do you have any questions?"

"Yes. Each floor has different visiting hours. Do you know what they are on this floor?"

"This is the Trauma Unit. Immediate family can come and go all day. The hours are three to four o'clock and then six to eight o'clock.

"What time is it now? I have my uniform on, so I can't take my arm out to look at my watch."

"It's exactly ten minutes to three. I'm going to check on Kristen now. She's in a private room, but they've placed another bed in the room with a female officer as the patient. I want to be sure everything is all set. Remember, this character has a large bandage on his left hand."

Sergeant Lewis lay perfectly still, thinking, *I hope they find a way to give me some coffee and get me to a men's room. This could be a long wait.*

The elevator doors opened. Dave Lewis tensed as he waited for people to walk within his view. Several older women walked by, being careful not to stare at him. Then an older couple. And floral delivery. He relaxed.

Mark stepped quietly into Kristen's room. He nodded at the private-duty nurse and pulled the paper mask off to show he was clean shaven. "Did Kristen open her eyes yet?"

"No, but she's been moaning in her sleep. That's a good sign."

Mark motioned to the additional bed, "Where's..?"

"In the bathroom taking a shower," indicating to the closed door.

Mrs Wheeler, are you sure you want to stay in here? We can place an officer..."

"I'm not leaving Kristen," she answered, emphatically, "and that's final."

The bathroom door opened quietly. "Were you speaking to me, Mrs Wheeler?"

Mark was surprised to see Ingrid Johansson standing in the bathroom doorway. "What are you doing here?"

"Well, they needed a female patient for the other bed. I figured why not me. There's no sense my waiting downstairs in my office all night when I can be up here in a comfortable bed."

"Captain," Mrs Wheeler smiled, "that's not the reason she gave me for being here."

"I'm sure of that, Mrs Wheeler," Mark grinned. "I didn't believe her for a minute."

Ingrid reached behind her to hold the hospital gown closed and hurried into the bed, pulling the sheet up at the same time.

"Don't you think you should have your slacks on under that thing, just in case anything happens?"

"As a matter of fact, I was just taking a shower and came out here to get dressed. As soon as you leave, I will."

"I was just leaving." Mark opened the door then turned to look at both women, "Thank you." He stepped out and closed the door.

Sergeant Lewis' gurney had been moved to the opposite side of the corridor and he now had a blue flowered cap over his hair. An intravenous bottle was hanging above him from a metal rod with a dummy tube hanging down and under the sheet.

Mark had to look closely as he walked toward him to be sure it wasn't a real patient and wondered what Dave would say if he knew they had put that flowery cap on his head.

The activity in the corridor looked natural — nurses entering and leaving rooms, visitors exiting the elevator.

"Everything all right, Dave?"

"Yes, nothing unusual."

Mark continued to walk past the gurney toward the nurses' station. He sat down, pretending to look at a patient's chart. The minutes ticked by slowly. His thoughts wandered.

***

"Would you like some coffee, doctor?"

Mark looked up and recognized one of his officers dressed in a nurse's uniform. "Yes, thank you."

As the nurse leaned toward Mark to place the cup in front of him, she whispered, "We're taking Sergeant Lewis into a room so he can have some coffee and stretch his legs. Will you be able to stay here to watch the corridor?"

"Ask him if he can wait five more minutes until the visiting hour is over and all the visitors have left the floor." Mark sipped his coffee, looked at his watch, decided to check on Kristen while the coffee cooled.

The charge nurse stopped him as he was leaving the area. "Doctor, could I speak to you in the conference room?" The nurse pointed to a door directly behind him. "There's a window so you can see out to the nurses' station and to the elevator area."

Mark followed the nurse into the room and closed the door. The nurse, thoughtfully, positioned herself with her back to the window so Mark could stand facing her and see through to the area beyond.

"This room is soundproof," the nurse assured Mark. "Dinner will start at four-thirty. We've arranged for dinners to be delivered for your staff to one of the empty rooms. If they eat in shifts, using that room, they won't have to leave the floor."

"That was very thoughtful of you," Mark smiled, continuing to look over her head watching the visitors as they entered the elevator.

"I didn't arrange it," the nurse replied. "My friend, Ingrid Johansson did. She's taking care of everything from her bed using her cell phone."

"Your friend?" Mark asked, surprised.

"Yes, she's my roommate."

"She's certainly in a strange profession."

"She attended the police academy."

"Yes, Mr. Fitzgerald told me. I was thinking of asking her to join my department."

"Oh, I don't think she'd do that...."

"Why not?" Mark asked, surprised.

"She was brutally raped two weeks before she was to graduate from the academy."

"I didn't know that."

"The rapist was caught and brought in to the station. Ingrid identified him, but as is the case, the rape victim is made to look like a tramp. And the rapist goes free. Ingrid thinks he's the one who's been doing all these rapes. She's very bitter about it."

"I don't wonder that she's bitter..."

"She can never get married because of it."

"Why not?" Mark asked, but kept looking through the window. "Does she hate men that much?"

"No, that's not the entire reason. He raped her with a broken bottle. It's not well known, but she and Doctor Bagley were engaged to be married."

"Jesus Christ," Mark muttered under his breath as he looked at the nurse. *That's why he's cognizant of what's going on. He went through the same thing.* "I better get her out of that room."

"I wouldn't do that if I were you. It's important for her to be there...to help Miss Miller."

"You're sure? I hope I haven't placed her in..."

"Yes, I'm sure. It's important for her to help get this guy. I have to give out medications now. After your staff has their dinner break and the patients' trays have been cleared from the floor, my staff will take their usual supper shift, two at a time, in the cafeteria."

Mark watched two well-dressed women talking as they waited for the elevator. The doors opened and the only person was the floral delivery guy with two arrangements. He stepped back to make room for the ladies. No one got off. The doors closed.

"Thank you," he smiled quickly glancing at her name tag, "Ms. Billings. You and your staff have been very helpful during this... Who's that?"

The nurse turned to see a man in a wheelchair, dressed in a hospital gown and gray hospital robe with a blanket over his legs, coming off the elevator. He looked nervously left then right, hesitated, then proceeded down the corridor towards Kristen's room.

"That can't be him," the nurse said, "he doesn't have long hair."

Mark pulled the door open, "Maybe he had a haircut or maybe he sent someone else." As he ran through the nurses' station, the elevator doors opened and Mark caught a glimpse of two floral arrangements being delivered as he was running toward the wheelchair.

"Hold on there, cowboy, where are you headed?"

"I'm lost. I'm looking for my room."

Several nurses from Mark's staff came running.

"What room number are you looking for?" Mark asked.

"I can't remember," he answered, wondering why all these people were looking at him. "I left my floor when the nurses weren't looking. I wanted to go down to the cafeteria for some ice cream. And now I can't remember..."

"What's your name?" Mark asked.

"I don't want to tell you. I don't want to get into trouble. They might throw me out of the hospital," the man answered, visibly shaken.

Kristen's door opened just wide enough for Ingrid to look out. "Is he the one you're looking for?" she asked Mark.

"No, but there might be more than one."

"Look at his wrist and see if he has a plastic hospital identification bracelet on," Ingrid whispered.

Mark reached for the man's wrist, but the man dropped his arm down beside the wheelchair. Mark leaned over the chair to grab the man's arm, knocking the blanket onto the floor. Mark stood up immediately. The man had no legs, they were cut off at the knees.

"Cover him up and get Nurse Billings," Ingrid instructed, as she quietly closed the door.

Mark beckoned the charge nurse, then apologized to the man and went looking for Sergeant Lewis. *He must be in a room having coffee.* Shaken and embarrassed, he turned to where he had left his coffee and took a sip. It was lukewarm. "Where's the coffee pot?" he asked the student nurse sitting at the desk.

"In the Utility Room," she replied, pointing toward the door.

Mark quickly refilled his cup and walked toward Sergeant Lewis who was now parked near the water bubbler. As Mark passed the nurses' station, he overheard a volunteer candy striper explaining to a nurse, "But Mrs Wainright says they aren't her flowers. She doesn't know anyone by the name on the card."

"Well, be careful to deliver them to the right person. This is the second time it's happened this afternoon."

"But I didn't deliver them," the young girl protested. "Mrs Wainwright told me a delivery man placed them on her night stand."

Mark would never know what made him turn around. This was none of his concern. "Is there a problem?"

"No," the nurse answered, "it's just that these flowers were delivered to the wrong patient. The florists are not supposed to bring them directly to the room. They've been told to leave them on that table over there and the candy stripers will deliver them to the patients."

*Oh no, the florist. He's been on and off this floor all afternoon. But he didn't have a bandage on his left... He was holding flowers...* Mark turned and ran toward Sergeant Lewis.

"Dave, the florist, the man who's been delivering the flowers. Did you see his left hand?"

Dave Lewis thought a moment, "No, he was carrying flowers, but his hair was short..."

"Yes, neat and newly cut. He came on the floor when I was running after the guy in the wheelchair." Mark ripped off the surgical mask and threw it on the floor. "Did you see him leave?"

"I was in a room having coffee and using the facilities when all that happened. I didn't see him."

"Dave, get off that stretcher. If it's the guy with the flowers, he could still be here. Get the others while I check Kristen's..."

A gunshot thundered from the opposite end of the corridor. They looked at each other and started to run toward Kristen's room. Mark was yelling instructions as he was running, "Keep everyone off this floor. Keep all patients in their rooms." He reached inside the back of the baggy green pants and gripped his service revolver just as a second explosion reverberated off the walls. Mark and Dave burst into the room, guns ready. Kristen was sitting up in bed trying to stop the flow of blood from Mrs Wheeler's shoulder as she lay slumped over Kristen's legs.

Mark indicated with his gun toward the curtain that was drawn around Ingrid's bed. In rapid pantomime he instructed Dave to whip open the curtain while he took aim at whatever they might encounter.

Dave reached for the curtain...

"Go ahead you bastard," Ingrid said, "Move again and I'll blow another part of you away. You'll never rape anyone again."

Mark nodded his head, silently indicating to Dave to open the curtain.

Ingrid was standing on the bed astride the man lying face up, writhing in agony, staring wide eyed at the revolver Ingrid was aiming directly at his face.

Mark could see the man's hands holding his genitals, or what was left of them. The bandage on his left hand was soaked with blood, as was the bed in between his legs.

"And now, bastard, even if you get away with this one," Ingrid snarled, "with a technicality in our lousy judicial system, you..."

"Ingrid," Mark said softly, it's over. You can get down now, we'll take it from here."

Ingrid hesitated, then slowly looked toward Mark.

"Come on, it's over," he said quietly, with a reassuring smile. He saw the tears erupt and flow down her face. "Dave, help her down and take her out of here. Send someone in to look at Mrs Wheeler." Mark kept his gun aimed at the man, although he was now unconscious, either from the pain or loss of blood. Mark really didn't care which, but he wasn't taking any chances.

"Mark," Kristen calmly stated, "that man shot this woman."

"Yes, I know he did," Mark answered, surprised at Kristen's calmness and her reference to 'that man'. *Hopefully, she has total memory loss of what she's gone through.* He stared at her somnolent eyes and knew she was still in shock, perhaps only awakened from her semi-coma by the gun shot, or perhaps her subconscious recognition of 'that man'.

Sergeant Lewis gave instructions to the officers gathered at the door to clear the room, as he assisted Ingrid out the door and into the corridor.

Two orderlies came in with a gurney to get Mrs Wheeler. As soon as she was rushed out of the room, another set of orderlies, actually police officers dressed as orderlies came in to take the prisoner away.

As soon as the prisoner was placed on the gurney, strapped down and wheeled from the room, Mark turned to Kristen and held her.

"Mark, why are you dressed like a doctor? Why am I in a hospital?" Kristen asked, as he cradled her in his arms, waiting for the nurses to return to care for her.

"It's a long story, darling, I'll tell you later, but first there's something I have to take care of."

"Please don't leave me, Mark."

"I'll be right back. You're in good hands now, these nurses are going to move you to another room."

Mark closed the door and walked to the nurses' station. "Where did they take the prisoner?" he asked the charge nurse.

"I heard them say that they're taking him to the hospital at the prison. They don't want to take any chances of him getting away again. So I would imagine they're still down in the Emergency Room area waiting for a prison ambulance to transport him."

Mark ran to the stairwell, rather than waiting for the elevator. He had to get to them before the prisoner was removed from the hospital. He pushed a door open, almost knocking down a nurse. "Do you know where a prisoner would be waiting to be..."

"There was a big to-do at the door of the Emergency Room. This is Out-Patient."

"Where the hell is the Emergency Room?"

"Through that door," she snapped at him, wondering why a doctor didn't know where the Emergency Room was.

Mark hurried through the double door. He didn't recognize the four uniforms gathered in the corridor. "Where's the prisoner? I hope you didn't leave him alone."

"And who might you be?" one of the officers barked.

"I'm Captain Winslow." Mark was trying to reach into his back pocket for his identification. He looked down and saw that he was still wearing the baggy green pants and they were covered with blood. He pulled out his badge wallet.

"My apologies, Captain Winslow. The prisoner is in that room, sir."

Mark cautiously opened the door. A doctor dressed in scrubs was standing facing the prisoner with his back to the door. Mark stepped quietly into the room and closed the door. "Doctor?"

Doctor Bagley spun around and hid something behind his back.

"Is anything wrong, sir?"

"No, nothing's wrong. I was just making sure the prisoner was comfortable, not feeling any more pain." *Other than the fact that I killed him. Now he won't recover and go after another victim. And this stuff can't be traced in his system.* "But unfortunately he had a considerable loss of blood and expired just a few minutes ago."

"Doctor Bagley, will you be signing the death certificate?"

"Yes, I can do that. No sense bothering the ME. He died in the hospital."

"Thank you." *Little does he know I came to do the same thing. I'm only sorry he got to him first.*

Mark turned, opened the door and stepped into the corridor. “This prisoner is dead. Return to your regular duties.”

Doctor Bagley slipped the hypodermic into his pocket when Mark wasn’t looking.

“I’ll go up and see how Kristen is doing.”

“And I have a few patients to see.”

# Chapter Sixteen

"Good morning, Mark. I waited in the corridor to speak with you."

"Good morning, Edward. Is..."

"Kristen is fine. I'm going to sell the Park Avenue apartment."

"Does Kristen know about that?"

"She's the reason I'm selling it. She says she can't go back there. And I don't blame her. It will be all I can do to go there and pack my office and a few belongings. Roland is going to help me. I'll sell it furnished.

I asked Mrs Ross, the housekeeper, to pack Kristen's things. She said she would do it as long as someone stayed with her. Roland will stay with her and he'll know what to pack other than her clothing. Marlene can't bring herself to do it."

"I'm just going in and visit with Kristen and then I'm going to attend Carol Bennett's funeral."

"That's where Marlene and I are going. Roland is driving. Why don't you join us? I have the Cadillac so there's plenty of room."

"Just give me a few minutes and I'll be right with you."

"Take your time, Mark. Marlene and I will wait down in the lobby. There's plenty of time before we have to be at the funeral home."

Mark went to Kristen's room and looked in to see if she was awake. The bruises on her face were beginning to change to yellow. Bottles and tubes were hanging everywhere.

She saw him through the slits in her eyes, the swelling was beginning to go down.

"Hi. You're all dressed up. Do you have court this morning?"

Mark carefully kissed Kristen on her forehead. It was the only place he dared touch. "Yes, court. I only have a few minutes, can't be late. But I'll come back right after." He gave her a big smile. "How are you feeling?"

"A little better, but very weak. Mark, I want to tell you something."

He sat on the edge of the bed and held her fingers that were sticking out of the bandages around a board to keep the IV tubes from falling out.

"I don't know how to say this."

Mark smiled. "Sometimes it's just easiest to get right to the subject." He held his breath, hoping her father hadn't talked her into going to Virginia.

"I'm pregnant."

Mark kissed her fingers and smiled. "I know."

"How do you know?"

"Doctor Bagley let the cat out of the bag thinking that I already knew."

"I hope you're not upset about it."

"Sweetheart, I couldn't be happier. I love you. And I can't wait to find out if it's a boy or girl."

"We'll have to think about names for either boy or girl."

She started to cry. "Mark, I thought I was going to lose the baby when..."

Mark squeezed his thumbnail into his palm and tried to smile. "You saved the baby. You're the bravest gal I know." Mark grabbed a tissue and wiped her eyes. And then his own.

"Oh Mark, now my nose is running and I've got these stupid boards on my hands holding all these stupid needles."

Mark wiped her nose. "Hey, look at me. *We're* going to have a baby. And *we're* going to get married right here in this hospital room."

"But I have my wedding gown. And Pamela has her dress."

"We'll have a big wedding later, if you want. If we're going to be thinking about girls' names and boys' names, we can't be guessing at the baby's last name. It won't work. Does Mickey go with Miller or Winslow? See what I mean? Or does Minnie go with Winslow or Miller? It just doesn't work. We're going to need a last name."

"Stop, it hurts when I laugh."

Mark checked his watch. He didn't want to make Marlene and Edward wait too long. "I can't be late for court."

"Mark, I'm not going back to the apartment. I can't."

"And I wouldn't want you to. Let's get married and we'll be a family in New Rochelle."

Kristen smiled. "I'd finally have a white picket fence."

Mark breathed a sigh of relief.

Kristen's voice was a little shaky, he knew she was exhausted. "I'm a little upset that Carol hasn't called or come to visit me. Mark, you just made a face, what's wrong, is she sick?"

"No, she's working on a case that has her out straight. I forgot to tell you she sends her love. Now I have to get going. I'll be back. You get a list of names ready. Mrs Wheeler will write them down for you. I'll be back later. Do your homework."

Mark rang for the nurse. "When I get back I want to tell you about an idea I have." Mark stepped outside the room. Mrs Wheeler, the private duty nurse, was hurrying down the hall.

"She asked about her friend Carol. I told her that she was straight out working a case. Now I'm off to Carol's funeral."

"Go ahead, Mark. I'll take care of her. You look very nice, by the way."

***

At the cemetery, Mark spoke quietly with the law firm partners. Kristen's secretary introduced him to a few other people from the firm. Then he waited until the last guest had spoken to Joshua Bennett.

"Joshua, what are your plans?"

"I'm going back to Dubai and try to get my mind off of this. If I stay here... No, I can't stay here, I know that. I'm going to sell the apartment. I've been staying at a friend's house. He helped me pack my clothes, a few personal items, and a couple of pictures. I saw the room where they..." Joshua started to cry and Mark held him close. "I was going to come back for the trial, but I can't even do that. I'd bring a gun and then I'd be in prison."

Mark whispered, "There isn't going to be a trial, they're both dead."

"Are you sure?"

"Positive. I want you to take my card, I've put my house and ranch phone numbers on it. If you ever need anything, or just to talk, a few drinks, a place to live, a horse to ride, you call me. Kristen and I are getting married, she's pregnant. We're going to live in New Rochelle. If Kristen agrees, as soon as she's stronger we'll move back to the ranch in Montana."

Suddenly, Joshua stopped crying and wiped at his eyes. He stood back, looked up at Mark and smiled. "Pregnant? I am so happy for both of you. You've given me something to live for, to look forward to. Now I can go back to Dubai and finish my work there." He managed a shaky smile. "Keep looking over the mountain top, because one day I'll be riding to the ranch to see that baby. You'll see me in a year or two."

"I'll hold you to it."

***

"Mrs Wheeler said you'd just had pain meds so if you feel up to it, let me run a couple of ideas by you. We'll have the small wedding. And when you're strong enough we'll go to Montana, for the honeymoon. And I'm thinking if you really like it there, we could live on the ranch."

"Could I have my own horse?"

"Sweetheart, you can have any damn thing you want."

"Could Mickey or Minnie have their own horse?"

Mark laughed and wondered just how much medication they had given her.

Kristen tried not to laugh.

"My other idea is, I was thinking that Mrs Ross doesn't have a job or a place to live. Right now she's living with her daughter. What do you think about asking if she'd like to work for us and live at the house? There are four bedrooms, so we have plenty of room. She can cook. She'd be there when you get home from the hospital. And I wouldn't have to ship Pamela to and from Connecticut. *And* she can cook."

"That's a wonderful idea. Let's call her right now and ask."

"Well, you're easy to please. Do you remember her phone number?"

"No. Call my dad; either he'll know it or his secretary will. If it's the secretary, I might have to speak to her, she won't give the number out to anyone she doesn't know."

Mark made the calls, got the number. Then called Mrs Ross, ran the idea by her, then had to wait for her to stop crying.

"I could come and get you, drive you to the house so you can see the house and where you'd be living."

"No, Captain Winslow, I don't have to see it."

"Okay. Do you know when you'd be able to move in? I'll come and get you and your things when you're ready."

"I'll be ready at five thirty."

Mark scrunched his eyebrows together. "Five thirty? What day or date, Mrs Ross?"

"Today."

"You want me to pick you up at five thirty today?"

"If that's a good time for you, yes. And Captain Winslow, you will deduct the thirty dollars I owe you from my first paycheck."

Mark chuckled. "Mrs Ross, what's your address? I'll be there at 5:30." He smiled and gave the thumbs up to Kristen. He wrote down the address and hung up the phone. "Can you believe that? We've got a live-in housekeeper and cook."

Kristen smiled. "I think 'cook' is the operative word here."

"Oh no, I didn't ask about the wage she expects."

"She'll have room and board, so it won't be as expensive as you think." *And if it is, the senator will kick in a few bucks.*

"Then what do we do with her if you decide you'd like to live in Montana?"

"She can either go with us or there's plenty of room at my parents' house."

"If we do decide on Montana, I could see if the sheriff's job is available, or a deputy's. And if you wanted to work, eventually, you could open a law office in Phillipsburg."

"I'd have to pass the Montana Bar."

"There's plenty of bars to pass in Montana, but I like to go in them."

They both laughed.

"I'd rather stay home with the baby."

“Then that’s what you will do. Whatever you want. I think you’d like it there. It’s a whole different way of life. It’s a little slower, a little less expensive to live, and everyone is friendly. It snows from September until June. One year we had eight inches of snow on July 4th, but that didn’t stop us, we still had the town cookout at the ball field; everyone had their grills and lounge chairs.

“I thought you told Justin you had never had a cookout in snow?”

“In the winter. This was July 4th.” And we waited until eleven o’clock for the fireworks to be set off on the side of the mountain.”

“Why that late?”

“That’s when it gets dark enough to see them.”

“You’re pulling my leg.”

“Nope. It’s true. It’s in the Rocky Mountains, one mile above sea level. The air is very dry so you hardly feel the cold. And the snow is light and fluffy. They don’t plow the roads, everyone drives over them with four-wheel drive trucks or snowmobiles. Phillipsburg has one main street with stores and restaurants. And the most wonderful candy store where they make their own candy.

An old smelter town next to it, Anaconda, is famous for having the tallest stack in America. And the tallest slide. It has the Washoe Theater that was voted by the Smithsonian Institute as the fifth most beautiful theater in America, in original condition; and only costs three dollars to see a movie. The Chamber of Commerce has a tour bus that takes the tourists to all the sites and a narrator that takes them inside. There's lots of restaurants and shops and bars and churches.

When you travel in the winter, you have to check with the mountain passes to be sure they're open. One time I was the last one through the pass before they closed it or I wouldn't have made it to the Amtrak station in Shelby."

"You really loved living there."

"I miss it like I would miss my right arm."

"Where will we stay if we go there?"

"I have a big house on the ranch just waiting for a family to move in."

"I hope your parents like me."

"Kristen, they love you already. Gail has filled them in where I left off. And my dad was here to see you the first day."

"What? I didn't know that."

"You were in a coma."

"If we have a small wedding here, could Pamela wear her pretty dress?"

"That would really make her happy. Thank you for thinking of it."

"Oh Mark, this is wonderful. It makes me so happy. I wish I could hug you right now."

"You let me know when you feel up to it and I'll make all the arrangements. Now, I better go find Mrs Ross."

# Chapter Seventeen

Mark pulled into his driveway thinking this could very well be the last trip they'd ever have to make between this house and his in-laws' in Connecticut.

Pamela opened her door and started walking to the house.

"Hey, there's a lot here to carry."

"Oh, I forgot," she said, hurrying back to the car. "I'm very tired so I can only carry one thing."

"Okay. I'll leave the things you'll carry right here. After you carry your one thing in, then come back and carry one more thing until you've emptied the trunk. I'm exhausted so I'll carry all this in one trip."

"Daddy, I'm really tired. Could you just bring everything in? That's what dads are for, carrying things."

Mark laughed. She was always one step ahead of him. He had to think fast. "Okay, I'll carry as much as I can, then I'll lock the trunk so no one can take your stuff. Later, when it's dark and you need anything out of the trunk, there's a flashlight near the back door."

Pamela stamped her foot knowing she had lost this argument. "Fine," she stated. "At least gram makes gramps carry everything."

"Yes, I know. That's why you like staying there, they treat you like a princess."

When they finally had everything out of the trunk and into the house, Pamela made a great show of collapsing onto a kitchen chair. "Daddy, are you going to marry Kristen?"

"Yes, I am. Do you have a problem with that?"

"No. But I was thinking then she could tell you to carry everything in the house."

"You can get that thought right out of your head."

"I really like Kristen. I just was thinking about where we'd live. Will I still live with you?"

"Pumpkin, you will always live with me. Is that what you're worried about?"

"A little."

"I think more than a little, you've been a grumpy Gus lately." Mark hugged his daughter while he jammed his thumbnail into his palm to keep the emotions away. "Gosh, I didn't know you were thinking about things. Is there anything else you'd like to know, or that's worrying you? You do know you can ask me anything, so if you're wondering about anything else..."

"Is Kristen going to be my mother?"

"Well, you'll always have a birth mother, but Kristen will be your mother." Mark knew he wasn't explaining this very well, but wasn't sure if..."

"Good, because I needed one. All the kids in school have a mother and they tease me, because I don't have one."

"Oh, sweetie, I didn't know that kids were teasing you. I would have gone shopping sooner and found one for you if I knew you *needed one*."

Pamela giggled. "I'm glad you waited, because now we have a good one. I'm trying to think of what I should call her. Mummy is for little kids, so I think I'll call her Mom. Do I have to wait until we marry her, or can I call her mom now?"

"I think now would be good. But you do what you feel comfortable, uh, what you feel you want to do."

"I like the name, Mom, that's what I'll call her. She looks like a nice mom, too."

"Sweetie, are you a little nervous about the whole thing, getting married, getting a mom?"

"Nervous?"

"Jittery."

"The most thing I feel is happy."

Pamela put her hands on her father's cheeks and looked him in the eyes, "Do you feel jittery?"

"A little. I feel jittery like Jell-O."

Pamela giggled. "What are you going to call Kristen after we marry her?"

Mark pretended to wonder what he should call her. "I think I'll call her Sugar Plum Honey Bunny."

Pamela pretended to fall on the floor and laughed. "Daddy, you are sick."

"Come here, sit on my lap for a minute. I want to tell you something."

"Uh-oh."

"What do you mean uh-oh?"

"When you want me to sit on your lap, you have something to tell me that I don't want to hear."

Mark laughed. "Get over here." He lifted Pamela to sit in front of him and hugged her to him. "This is about...your mom. She was in a little accident..."

Pamela whipped her head around. "What happened? Is she okay? She's still gonna be my mom, right?"

"Oh yes, that's all the same, but she's in the hospital and will be there for a while, so we have to cancel the big wedding and have a small wedding in her hospital room. But you can wear your new long dress."

Pamela jumped down. "Okay."

Mark chuckled to himself, *I guess the operative words here are — 'long dress'.* "What do you say we go out to have pizza for supper and then stop for ice cream cones afterward?"

Pamela hugged him, "Yes, that's the best idea."

Mrs Ross came into the kitchen in her yellow chenille robe. "I thought I heard noise down here. Did you have a good time, Pamela?"

"Yes, but I'm happy to be home. We're going for pizza and ice cream, would you like to come with us?"

"No thank you, dear, I already ate."

"Mrs Ross, do you need anything while we're out?"

"Not a thing, Mark. You two have a good time."

"It will probably be dark by the time we get back, so I'll lock the door. We're stopping for ice cream on the way back..."

Mrs Ross turned around and smiled, "Maple walnut." Then turned around again and headed back upstairs to her room.

Mark locked the door and started down the porch steps.

"Hello Mark." April, the single neighbor, who had moved in last year, sashayed toward him with enough cleavage showing that he wondered why she even bothered wearing a top. "I saw you carrying in all the beach chairs and toys. Been to the beach?"

*No, I just like hauling all this crap around.* "Yes, Pamela was visiting her grandparents."

"Oh, what fun. Have you had dinner yet? I made a pot roast this afternoon, if you'd like to come over."

"Well, that's very nice of you, but we're just going for pizza and..."

"Guess what, Miss April, dad and me are getting married."

"Oh, you're so cute. But you can't marry your father," she laughed.

"*I'm* not marrying daddy. Daddy and me are marrying Kristen."

"Oh how nice. Is that so, Mark?"

"Yes, April, you've probably seen her here a few times."

"Oh, that woman with the Corvette?"

"That's the one," Pamela chided.

Mark looked at Pamela and started to laugh, but covered it with a cough. "We better be going. Thank you for the dinner invitation, that was very thoughtful." He was sure he heard her say, It's the last one you'll get. But he was probably mistaken.

Pamela was sitting in the car with her hands folded in her lap and a devilish smile on her face.

"You were a little rude, Pamela. Don't you like her?"

"Not really, because when gram and gramps were here last time, gram told gramps that she was sure the neighbor, April, was trying to get her hooks in you."

Mark burst out laughing and chuckled all the way to Tony's Pizza Parlor.

***

Mark checked the hospital chapel to be sure everything was ready. With all the white calla lilies and roses on the altar, it looked like Queen Elizabeth was due to arrive. There were twelve pews, six on each side and someone had attached large white bows at the ends of them.

A few guests were already seated. The law partners and their wives, Kristen's secretary and her husband. Probably a few people from the Miller family. Most of Mark's crew were there. Just enough people to make it look like a wedding. Kristen would be pleased.

Mark had asked Mrs Ross to sit in the front row on the groom's side with Jessica's parents, knowing that if she sat on the bride's side she'd be pushed to the back like a servant. Then he had asked Alice and Henry Clark, Jessica's parents, to represent his family because they couldn't be here. Explaining that Mrs Ross, who had watched over Kristen for the past six years like a mother hen, would be alone. Each one thought they were keeping the other company.

"Daddy, daddy, over here."

"Oh, there you are... Sweetie, you look beautiful."

Pamela twirled around in her long dress with a grin from ear to ear. "And I'm wearing the locket Kristen gave me for being her flower girl."

Mark gave it a closer look, even though he had purchased it the day before. "That is beautiful. Be sure to thank her."

Mark thanked Alice and Henry for coming and staying with Pamela.

"We're happy to be here, Mark."

"I really appreciate it. You'll always be our family."

"You look very nice," Alice whispered. I'm wondering, since Pamela is wearing a long dress, is Kristen wearing a wedding gown?"

"Yes. The bridal shop cut it down the back and fixed it so they could just lay it over Kristen in front and attach it in back so it will look like she's wearing it.

And Pamela, let me just remind you of a couple of very important things. When you see Kristen, be sure to smile. Her face is bruised and we wouldn't want her to feel sad."

"I promise. Gram helped me practice in the mirror yesterday."

"Your job is to walk in front of the wheelchair, smiling, remember to always smile. And sprinkle the rose petals in the aisle as you walk to the front. When you get to the front, just like we practiced, you'll walk over and sit with gram, gramps and Mrs Ross. Okay?"

"Got it."

"That's my girl."

Mark saw the commissioner come in with his wife and sit on the bride's side. Ah, politics.

"Kristen's mother and father have arranged for a dinner after the wedding. You will go with gram, gramps and Mrs Ross to the restaurant for dinner. I've ordered a special plate for you, chicken sticks and fries. Daddy and Kristen won't be able to go, because Kristen has to stay in the hospital. When gram, gramps and Mrs Ross are ready to leave, you go home with them and stay with Mrs Ross. And gram and gramps if they stay over night. And I'll see you tomorrow. I'm going to stay with Kristen tonight. We're going to have dinner in her room."

"Got it."

"Okay. I see Kristen coming. You go over to the chapel door and wait there for her. Remember not to look surprised. I have to go up front and wait for both of you to come down the aisle. Where's your basket of rose petals?"

"Right there on a chair by the door. "Daddy." Pamela beckoned to him with her finger and pointed to her cheek.

Mark bent down and kissed her.

Pamela held his face and whispered, "Don't be jittery like Jell-O." Then she turned and hurried to the chair to get the basket and waited for Kristen.

Mark's jitters had suddenly vanished. He nodded and smiled his way to the front of the chapel, stopped and spoke with Marlene and Ed. Ed had conceded to not wheel Kristen down the aisle so that Doctor Bagley could be in attendance at all times. Kristen would be momentarily off her IVs so that she didn't have to "wear them" for the wedding.

Doctor Bagley pushed Kristen's wheelchair to the chapel entrance. Mrs Wheeler, Kristen's private duty nurse walked down the aisle, winked at Mark to let him know everything went as planned, and sat on the groom's side in the second pew.

Pamela walked to stand in front of Kristen and smiled. "Hi Mom, you look beautiful."

Kristen's eyes started to fill. She leaned forward, pressed his thumbnail into her palm and hugged Pamela. "Thank you, my daughter. You look beautiful, too. Are you ready?"

Pamela smiled, "Yes, I'm ready. Thank you for the locket that you gave me for being the flower girl." Pamela turned and started tossing rose petals. Mark forgot to tell her to walk slow. She smiled at her dad, went to sit in the front pew, put the basket down, and straightened her dress.

As Doctor Bagley pushed the wheelchair to the front, there were a few gasps from people who hadn't seen Kristen. He parked the chair to the left of a chair that had been placed there for Mark to sit in so he wasn't towering over her. Then went and sat in the second pew on the groom's side with Mrs Wheeler.

Mark smiled at Kristen, kissed her and sat in the chair beside her, taking her hand.

And Pamela walked up and stood beside Kristen on the left side. Not as planned.

When the minister asked who gives this woman... Edward stood up and said, "Her mother and Pamela and I do."

Pamela turned, looked at Edward and smiled.

And Mark thought, *Oh good God, I'll bet that wasn't Ed's idea.*

It was going to be a very quick service, because they weren't sure how long Kristen could sit up in the wheelchair. The minister asked Mark, "Do you take this woman to be your lawfully wedded wife?"

Mark opened his mouth to answer and Pamela spoke up very loudly and said, "We do."

The guests tried to laugh quietly.

And Mark said, "We do."

Kristen turned and kissed Pamela, then turned to Mark and kissed him.

And Alice and Henry tried to hold it together.

When it was time for the married couple to go back down the aisle, Kristen whispered to Pamela, "Get on my lap very carefully. Then looked up at Mark, "Okay husband, we're ready."

The guests stood and applauded.

And Mark heard the commissioner say, "This is the most enjoyable wedding I've ever been to."

***

Kristen was back in bed with all her tubes hooked up. They were waiting for their dinner to be served.

"Mark, you looked so handsome in your tuxedo. And Pamela was delightful. When I entered the chapel she came right to me and said, "You look beautiful, Mom." I almost started to cry but I used your thumbnail trick. And she thanked me for the locket.

And just so she doesn't get in trouble with you, I had asked my father to call her when you weren't home and find out if she'd like to say or do anything during the wedding. She had two requests, that she be able to stand beside us... She told dad, 'I want three of us together when we get married, we're going to be family and I'm going to live with them.' Then dad told her that he was going to be her grandfather and Marlene would be her grandmother. I'm not sure how he explained that to her, but then she asked him how many grandparents would that be, because she already has grandparents. Dad got such a kick out of her. He told her six grandparents."

Mark laughed, "And she was probably counting how many Christmas and birthday gifts she'd be getting. And that was very nice of you to think of that. She really wanted to be a part of it."

"It was dad's idea to include her in the giving away part. I don't think she understood the giving away, but I'm sure having her name mentioned was special for her."

"You looked beautiful today. And your gown looked like you were wearing it. I think the photographer got a lot of pictures."

"I didn't know there was going to be a photographer. I don't want pictures."

"Sweetheart, he's going to airbrush them. And do two parents' albums. How are you feeling?"

"A little worn out. Would you mind if I rest a while? You could go to the restaurant and eat and then come back."

"No, Mrs Winslow, I'll stay here with you. They're bringing our dinner in later. You take a little snooze and I'll go down to the cafeteria and bring back a cup of coffee. Do you want anything?"

"A kiss would be nice."

"That I can handle." Mark was careful not to get tangled in the tubes and gave her a warm lock lips kiss, the first one in a very long time.

"Wow, that should hold me until you get back."

"Get some sleep, I'll get some coffee and stop at the newsstand and grab a paper to read."

"Mark, you know we won't be able to do anything, you know, anything for quite a while, maybe months."

"I know that, sweetheart. I don't care if it's years, so don't worry about it. As long as we're together."

Kristen's eyes filled... "Go on, go get coffee while I stay here and feel sorry for myself."

"You can get that thought right out of your head. There's nothing to feel sorry about. You just think positive, think about the baby, think about names, and get better. By the way, where is that list of names? We can work on that later."

Kristen smiled. "How long can you stay?"

"It's our wedding night. They're going to bring another bed in after we eat. I'll push them together and we can canoodle all night."

"Canoodle?"

Mark could still hear Kristen laughing when he stepped into the elevator. It was so good to hear her laugh again. *I'll call Dave and ask him to swing by with two pieces of wedding cake for us when he and Cheryl leave the restaurant.*

# Chapter Eighteen

"Now that you're out of the hospital, we should decide if we want to fly to Montana, take the train, or drive. If we fly we can be there in one day, but it makes for a very a long day. There's the hassle of going through TSA, standing in line, take off your shoes, no jewelry, no belt buckles, things like that. Long walks down a ramp to the plane, long flights, no meals, no leg room, no arm room, babies crying, kids kicking the back of your seat. Change planes in Minneapolis. They have golf carts to take you from one gate to the next, but it's a long wait for the next plane and if the first plane is late, then you miss the second plane. And from there we take a much smaller plane that I have to duck my head to walk in."

"Mark, I don't want to fly. I, I don't want those TSA people touching me. I'm sorry, I can't do it." Kristen started to cry. She was trembling.

Mark jumped out of his chair and held her. "Sweetheart, I'm so sorry. I should have thought of that. No flying. That's good, I hate flying."

"I'm sorry, Mark."

"Don't you be sorry. It's my fault."

"Is there another way?"

"Amtrak would take a couple of days travel, but it's fun, it's like being on a cruise. There's no TSA hassle, no waiting in long lines. We'd have two bedrooms; one for us and one for Pamela and Mrs Ross. The bedrooms have a bathroom and a shower. The sleeper car is next to the dining car. At night the porter comes in and sets up the beds. In the morning the porter serves you juice and brings a newspaper, asks what time you'd like to eat breakfast, then he comes and gets you when it's time. Then while you eat breakfast, he takes care of the beds. Or he'll deliver the food to the room if you don't feel like getting dressed. The food is excellent and the meals are included with the bedroom price."

"Would we be stuck in the bedroom the entire trip?"

"No, you can move anywhere in the train. There's a club car where they have movies and games for kids. And downstairs there's a snack bar. You sit in comfort and get to see the country. Oh, and there's plugs for a computer or whatever you want to plug in."

"You, obviously, want to go by train. It does sound nice."

"Actually, I'd rather drive. I was just trying to offer choices."

"How long would it take to drive to Montana?"

"It takes thirty-six hours, but that's driving straight through. We could have Triple-A map the trip so we'd have motels with the right amount of rooms and beds ready for us. And it's the cheapest and most comfortable way to go."

"We wouldn't all fit in your car."

"I was wondering if you'd be willing to trade in your Corvette for a van — which you'll need soon anyway. I've been looking at Chrysler Town and Country vans. They cost a little more than a Corvette, but you could get a good trade-in. The one I think you'd like is a seven passenger with DVD and television screens. There are separate screens for the middle and rear seats so not everyone has to watch the same movie. This van has everything except a kitchen sink. It even has a table stowed away that is easily set-up. And the seats swivel so you can sit at the table and eat or play games. The power slide smart doors stop and back up if something gets in the way, you know, like children. Give it some thought and let me know what you decide."

"Let's go shopping for a van this afternoon."

Mark laughed. "You're so easy to please."

"Now, what about Mrs Ross?"

"I did tell her we're planning a trip to see if we, meaning you, would like to live there. I asked if she would like to come and have a look around and see if she'd like to live there with us."

Kristen held her breath. "What did she say?"

"Much the same as when we asked her to come here. She smiled and said, "I'll be packed and ready, just let me know what day we're leaving."

"Just like that?"

"Yes."

"That would be a blessing."

"I did ask if her children would be upset. She said, "They have their own lives. If they want to see me, they'll invite me and I'll come for a visit.'"

"I think that's why you like her so much, not just for her cooking. She's very matter-of-fact, doesn't hedge around."

"I think you're right. Did we get any mail today?"

"I put it on your desk. I opened the cards. There's a letter there, I think it must be your uncle or a relative, the return address says Albert Winslow."

"My uncle, the rich one. He's probably apologizing for not making it to the wedding." Mark went to his desk to get the letter.

Kristen finished writing a thank you note and was addressing the envelope.

"Sweetheart, you won't believe this. Uncle Albert heard we're going to Montana for a visit. While we're gone he's having decorators come in and give us a complete nursery."

"Oh my god, really? A complete nursery? Will he want to be the godfather or something?"

"No, that's not his way. He gives to give. Pop must have told him we were expecting. He even sent paint chips so you could pick out which color you want the room painted. Oh wait, there are chips here of wood samples for the furniture. And pictures of the furniture. There's a list of every gadget he's ordered. A crib, the bedding, the bumpers. A changing table on top of a bureau… Look, he's drawn an arrow showing the special side so the baby can't fall off. An armoire with little hangers. And the list goes on. Oh, and a year's supply of Pampers. And a special thing to put the dirty ones in. Wait, a heated thing for the baby wipes." Mark dissolved into laughter. "I'll let you read it."

"How will they get in if we're all in Montana?"

"He works for the CIA so he probably doesn't need a key, but I'll include one when we send him the paint chips."

"But what if we move to Montana?"

"Well, we'll take all the stuff and leave the paint on the walls."

"Smart ass." Kristen began to read the letter. "Mark, I didn't know we'd need all this stuff for a baby. Oh look, a special recliner rocking chair for the nursery. A monitor so we can hear him if he cries. Oh, a pram, an actual British pram. And a stroller with a thing that the baby sits in so you don't have to lift him out of one thing to put him in a car seat."

"When do you go for another jelly on the belly thing to make sure he's okay?"

"Jelly on the belly? Is that a new technical name for an ultrasound?"

"Well, that's what it looked like when they did it."

"They'll do another one during the next visit and that will be the last one."

"Remind me the day before so I can go with you. Have you picked out a middle name for the baby yet?"

"Yes, but maybe I should change it to Albert, since he's giving us a complete nursery."

"I think he'd be embarrassed if we chose his name. He'd feel that we felt obligated to choose his name. And that's not why he gives gifts."

"Okay, then I chose Allan A-L-L-A-N. Hunter Allan Winslow."

"I like it. Why or how did you come by the name Allan?"

"It's my mother's middle name. It's a Scottish last name."

"Your mother's middle name or your father's?

"My mother's."

"I do like it. The name flows."

"Let's go buy a van."

"I'll let Mrs Ross know we're going out and see if she needs anything."

"And remind her that Pamela will be home from school at three o'clock, just in case we're not back by then."

***

"Something smells good. Is that your famous meatloaf, Mrs Ross?"

"That it is," she smiled.

"What time is dinner?"

"Five o'clock. I planned it earlier than usual, because you said you wanted to talk tonight about the trip to Montana."

"Do you want me to set the table?"

"We're eating in the dining room, it's already set. I thought you might have papers and things you wanted to share so I thought that table would give you more space."

"Mrs Ross, if you ever leave you're taking me with you."

"Oh, go on with you," Mrs Ross laughed.

"Where are Kristen and Pamela?"

"They're upstairs working on homework."

Mark went to the bottom of the stairs, "Hi honey, I'm home."

Pamela called down, "Which honey do you mean?"

"I meant my sugar plum honey bunny."

He could hear Pamela giggling. "He means you, Mom."

Kristen laughed, "I'll be right down, Shrek. There's mail on your desk. The Triple-A trip planner pack came today."

Mark headed to his desk. He wanted to have everything set next to his place at the table so they could talk about the trip. He checked the map to be sure they had routed him on the longer route so he didn't have to see the place where Jessica and Todd were killed.

Kristen came down stairs. "Hi, honey, you're home early.

"Hi, gorgeous. I had an easy day today. How are you feeling? Mark stood up and hugged her.

"Very good." What's this about a sugar plum honey bunny?"

"Just before the wedding, when Pamela was deciding which name she would call you and decided on Mom, she asked me what I was going to call you when we got married. That was the only silly name I could come up with and she fell on the floor laughing. What did the doctor say today?"

"The baby is fine. They'll do a cesarean September 15th. Then they'll do the reconstructive surgery right after."

"The same day?"

"He said it would be better to get it all done at the same time, no sense healing from one and then going through another."

"Oh, I see. It's not because there's a problem or anything?"

"No, just for expedience sake and so they don't have to put me under twice in such a short time."

"Okay. Any worries? Are you jittery like Jell-O?"

"Not at all. I'll be so happy to get it done and over with."

Pamela yelled down from upstairs, "Dad?"

"What is it?"

"What's another word for fertile ground?"

Mark looked perplexed.

"She asked me the same thing. I didn't know what to tell her. Someone told her that the neighbor next door, April, is moving to more fertile ground."

Mark tried to laugh quietly. "Pamela, it means that April is going elsewhere with her hooks."

"Oh, okay."

"What!?"

"When you and I first started dating, Pamela overheard gram telling gramps that April was trying to get her hooks in me. And Pamela thinks they're real hooks. And I didn't correct her, because that would have led to a more in depth explanation."

"Oh. Now I understand why April would never speak to me."

"Dinner is ready."

"Mrs Ross, I'll help you carry everything in to the dining room." *At least I don't need a jackhammer for this meatloaf.*

Pamela smelled the food and came downstairs. "Are we going to talk about the trip after dinner? I can't wait to see Sweetie Pie. I should call her and tell her I'm coming. She'll be happy to hear that."

Mrs Ross looked bewildered. "Who is Sweetie Pie?"

"She's my horse."

"And you call and talk to her on the phone?"

"Yes."

"Does she talk to you?"

"Yes, of course."

Mark said, "Mrs Ross, my father takes the phone out to the barn so that Pamela can talk to Sweetie Pie."

Mrs Ross was no dummy, she picked up on it right away. "I can't wait to get there, I think this is going to be fun."

"My dad has a horse named Colorado and..."

"Does your dad talk to his horse on the phone?"

Mark said, "No, my father gets tired of holding the phone to the horses' ears."

Mrs Ross couldn't stop laughing. "I'm not going to be able to eat if this keeps up."

"So, about the trip. We'll leave the day after Pamela gets out of school. That's June 16$^{th}$. Two weeks from today. The trip is two thousand three hundred miles and it takes thirty-six hours. That would be if we drove straight through. But we'll stop at motels along the way. Everyone make a list of what you want to bring in the car, snacks, CDs, DVDs, neck pillow, light blanket, sweater or light jacket, books, handheld games and small things to keep busy while riding. And ranch clothes, nothing fancy; jeans, slacks, sweatshirts, socks. A few days before we go we can sit in the van and learn how to adjust the seats, how to play a movie, how..."

Pamela asked, "A movie, we can watch a movie in the van?"

"Yes, DVDs. And there are headsets for each person. We'll go through that when we learn about the car. On the way, we'll stop and eat in restaurants, that will give us a chance to stretch our legs, use the rest rooms, replenish the snacks. And we'll stay in motels at night. Oh, and we'll bring a cooler with bottled water and soda. Any questions?"

Mrs Ross asked, "How long are we going to stay?"

We'll stay there two weeks. I have three weeks vacation so we'll use the extra week for travel to and from.

"And where will we stay when we get there?" Mrs Ross asked.

"I have a five bedroom furnished house on the ranch. We'll stay there. My parents live in the big house. That's where the ranch hands eat. The ranch cook lives in that house. We'll probably have a few meals there. Mrs Ross, have you ever ridden a horse?"

"Yes, when I was younger, and I'm not too old to try it again. I rather enjoyed it."

"Do you, by chance, have a driver's license?"

"Yes, I have one."

"Would you mind sharing some of the driving on the trip?"

"It would be a pleasure. I haven't driven in a while, but it's like riding a bike, it comes back to you."

"I didn't know you had a license. You've never asked to use one of the cars."

"No, Kristen, they're not my cars. I would never ask."

"Mrs Ross, the cars in the driveway are yours to drive any time you want. Matter of fact, I have a truck in the garage. You'll have my car and I'll drive the truck."

"Well, not to be too pushy, but I'd prefer the truck, if you don't mind."

Mark laughed. "That works for me. The keys are on the hook by the back door. It's yours to drive, so please don't ask to use it every time. I'll get you a gas card."

"Oh no, I'll pay for my own gas."

"Well, get that thought right out of your head. Unless you take a long trip with it, I prefer to pay for the gas, because I know darn right well you'll be using it for errands for us most of the time."

"Then I'll say thank you. You are both very generous. You've provided a lovely and happy home to live in. And now a truck to drive. And now a trip to Montana."

"But Mrs Ross," Pamela piped up, "you cook us good food and desserts."

"Thank you."

"I think we covered everything about the trip. Pamela, would you help Mrs Ross clear the table and we'll have dessert."

Pamela stood without a fuss and began clearing the table. When Mrs Ross and Pamela were done clearing and in the kitchen, Kristen whispered to Mark, "I notice you never order Pamela to do something, you ask or suggest and it works every time. I admire that."

"It's something I grew up with. My parents never ordered us to do anything. They requested. My mother would say, 'Would you clean your room.' We knew she wasn't giving us choice, it was a request that we knew we should do. It was a polite way of telling us to clean our room. My father would ask us to clean the horse stalls, and we did it. They didn't boss us just because we were children, they treated us with respect and we lived up to that respect."

"But you said your mother would be cross with you if you stubbed your toes without shoes on."

"If my mother had previously asked us to never go barefoot, she would explain the reason she was asking. Then if we stubbed our toe without shoes on, she would take us to task by saying, 'Don't cry to me, you didn't have your shoes on.' She didn't put us down, or slap us. Matter of fact, I don't ever recall my parents hitting any of us. Because they treated us with respect, we were eager to please. Not to say we didn't cause trouble, we did our share, but that's all in part of growing up. We learned fast to never tell my mother we were bored with nothing to do, because she'd hand us a dust cloth and set us to dusting the dining room furniture, which had nooks and crannies in every part of the damn wood."

"Ahh," Kristen smiled, "she taught without lecturing."

"Not to say that I didn't get in trouble growing up. But she had a way of scaring the crap out of us by drawing a verbal picture of a punishment she'd do to us if we ever did it again. I remember one time she was so angry that she told me, 'I will put your head through that wall and while you're watching the horses run around out there I'll be on this side smacking your back end.' And I said, 'There aren't any horses on that side of the house.'"

Kristen looked shocked. "What did she do to you?"

"She laughed."

"You are kidding?"

"No." My mother's a saint. Sometimes I wonder why she let me live. Watch Mrs Ross, when they come back in, how she handles Pamela."

A moment later, "Now, here we are with dessert. Strawberry shortcake and Pamela did the beautiful swirls of whipped cream on top."

And Pamela smiled proudly, as though she had worked all day baking the biscuits, picking and slicing the strawberries plus whipping the cream.

And Mark, as usual stated, "My favorite dessert." When he really favored lemon meringue pie.

# Chapter Nineteen

The entrance to the ranch was marked by two massive peeled logs supporting a cross log with "**Ranch It'll Do**" carved deep into the wood. Lincolnshire fencing stretched for what looked like miles on each side of the ranch gate.

"Here we are, this is the road *on* the ranch that leads to the houses, you can see them over to the right in that copse of trees."

Mark turned onto the long road, rumbling across the cattle guard, then pointed to the right at the men on horses. Suddenly, one horse cut from the group and began racing toward the van.

Pamela shouted, "It's Grampa. Daddy stop, stop the car, I have to get out."

"I'll stop, but please wait until the horse stops before you go running to it."

"I will." Pamela opened the window as far as it would go and started waving, "Grampa, it's me, I'm here."

A giant of a man jumped down from the horse while it was still moving and ran toward the van.

Mark pushed the button to slide the side door open. "Okay, Pamela, you can get out."

"Grampa." Pamela ran to her grandfather and he picked her up and swung her around. Then hugging her close, "You're finally here. I'm so happy to see you."

Pamela hugged his neck tight. "And I'm happy to see you, too, Grampa. And guess what, I'm going to get a baby brother. Where's Sweetie Pie?"

"She's in the barn waiting to see you."

"Did you show her my picture in the pilgrim dress?"

"I did, and she wanted me to hang it up in her stall so she could look at it until you got here."

Mark got out and walked around the front of the van.

His father took Pamela's hand and walked her to his horse to allow the horse to catch her odor. The horse bumped her gently with his muzzle. "Look Grampa, he likes me."

Paul picked Pamela up and placed her on his saddle. He then hurried toward Mark. "Son, welcome home." They shook hands then turned to the van.

Kristen was having ten fits that Pamela was sitting by herself on that big horse. She opened the door to get out.

"Sit still, sit still, I'll come to you. You probably don't remember, but we already met. I was at the hospital and you were so excited to see me you slept right through my visit."

Kristen laughed, "I must have looked a site."

"I looked beyond the bruises and saw the prettiest gal I've ever seen. And you're even more beautiful now."

"Thank you. Is Pamela all right on that horse by herself?"

"Don't worry, that horse won't move unless I tell him to." Paul bent down and peered into the side door that Pamela had left open. "And you must be Mrs Ross. How do," he said, taking her offered hand into his large mitt.

"I do well, Mr. Winslow. This is a pleasure. Thank you for inviting me to your ranch."

"My name is Paul. And yours is?"

"Elizabeth, but they call me Betsy."

"Betsy, welcome to the ranch." Standing up, he said, "Okay, let's get to the house before the boss comes out with her shotgun. She's probably in the window now. I'll take Calamity Jane with me." And with that, he walked to his horse, jumped on behind Pamela and rode off at a gallop toward the house.

Mark got in the van. "Okay, you can put your hearts back where they belong," he laughed, "she's in good hands."

Mrs Ross pushed the button to slide the door closed.

Kristen turned her head toward the back seat, "I've known you for many years, Mrs Ross, and never knew your name is Betsy."

"I thought it was Elizabeth. At least that's what I write on your paychecks." Mark exclaimed, "Oh, Betsy, Betsy Ross."

"That's why I usually don't tell anyone my name."

Mark drove to the house where his mother was waiting on the porch, sans shotgun, but chomping at the bit. She hurried to the car and hugged her son the moment he was able to get the door open. "I hear from the grape vine, who rode by here a minute ago, that she's getting a baby brother." She knew what a baby boy would mean to her son.

She wiped her tears on her apron before meeting Kristen and Mrs Ross, then welcomed everyone into the house.

In the short time that they were in the big house, Kristen fell in love with her mother-in-law. And Gwendolyn and Betsy Ross became good friends.

***

"There's five bedrooms, a nursery, and three bathrooms and a sewing room upstairs. Downstairs there's the living room, dining room, breakfast room, kitchen with a pantry, den, office, playroom and bathroom. And a separate apartment off the kitchen for the cook. If we decide to live here, Mrs Ross, you have a choice of living upstairs or in the separate apartment off the kitchen."

"Do you mind if I look at the apartment?"

"You go right ahead, make yourself at home. It's furnished, but you can add whatever you want. I just don't want you to feel you have to live in the apartment and not feel part of the family. In other words, you'd have your meals with us. If we travel you would have the choice of whether to go with us or stay here." He smiled, "Like it or not, you are part of this family. While you look at the apartment, I'll show Kristen the upstairs."

Mark slowed his steps going up to the second floor so he didn't rush Kristen who was now almost seven months pregnant. "This is the master bedroom. We'll get a new bedroom set, if you want."

"That's not necessary. We'll have our own pillows and bedding."

"Whatever you want to do, it's up to you. It can't be easy moving into a house where another woman lived."

"I think it might be distressing if I didn't know she was such a wonderful person. This is us now and we can't be worrying about things that used to be. This room is gigantic."

"There's a walk-in closet. And a bathroom en suite. This door leads to the nursery. It was turned into Todd's... Sorry, it will take me a while to go in there."

Kristen thought, *Perhaps it will be easier for him once it's turned back into a nursery with our new nursery furniture from Uncle Albert.*

"Come on, I'll show you Pamela's room. If we move here you can change all the curtains and drapes, whatever to make it your own." He pulled Kristen gently into a hug.

"Mark, this is your house, not anyone else's. It's only bothering you, not me. So stop worrying. And I do want to move here."

"Really? You made up your mind already?"

I was thinking, I'd have the baby September 15$^{th}$, and the reconstructive surgery. Some recovery time and then we'd probably be able to move here in November."

"You've got it all figured out. You are one fantastic woman, Mrs Winslow. Come on, let's go see how Mrs Ross is doing."

Mrs Ross was already in the kitchen checking out the food situation. "Someone already filled the pantry. After a day or two, I'll probably find a few things we need. How close is a grocery store?"

"Not close, but there are small stores in town that might have what you're looking for. If not, we can drive to a big grocery store. Going to a store that isn't local is measured in miles if it's over an hour to get there. And minutes if it's under one hundred miles. There's a Wal-Mart Super store in Butte, about forty minutes. There are two big grocery stores in Anaconda, and that's about twenty minutes from here. Tonight we'll have dinner at the big house, that's my parents' house. Tomorrow we can think about groceries. As long as you have what you need for breakfast."

Mark looked out the window, "There goes Pamela on Sweetie Pie." They hurried to the window to see her.

"Should she by herself?"

"Don't worry about her, Kristen. Unless it's raining, you won't see her all day, any day. She stays with my father and the ranch hands. She thinks she's a cowgirl. You may think she's alone, but right now there's probably twenty sets of eyes watching her."

"What if she falls off the horse?"

"Well, I don't know about now that she's bigger, but a few years ago she fell off and couldn't get up. Sweetie Pie bit the back of her jeans, not Pamela, just the jeans and carried her home."

"In her teeth?"

"It wasn't that far, but we were amazed. The horse is like a faithful pet dog."

"I'm going upstairs and change, do a little riding before dinner. I'll stop in front of the house so you can meet Colorado."

"Okay. I'll help Mrs Ross unpack and get settled in."

"Why don't you sit on the porch and rest, Kristen. I can fly through this in no time. Then I'll come out and sit with you."

"I am a little tired. I'll just take a look around downstairs and then I'll be on the porch."

Kristen was settled with her feet up when Mrs Ross brought two cups of coffee and joined her. There was lots of activity, horses with riders went back and forth, tipping their hats to the ladies.

"Kristen, I hope you decide to move here."

"I've already decided. Will you come with us?"

"I wish I had found this place years ago. Yes, I will definitely love living here. I brought a pair of jeans with me so I'll try riding tomorrow."

"Oh, who is this handsome guy in that big cowboy hat. He's coming this way. Oh my god, that's Mark.

"I stopped so you could get to know Colorado."

"Mark, you took my breath away."

"Why, what..?"

"I didn't know it was you under that big hat."

Mrs Ross laughed, "She just said, Who's the handsome cowboy headed this way."

"We'll have to get both of you some western clothes. We'll go shopping tomorrow."

All I need is a cowboy hat and I'm ready to ride," Mrs Ross laughed.

Mark dismounted. "Kristen, just step down here so Colorado will know you."

"He's awfully big, I'll just stand back here."

"No, now come on, I'll hold your hand. Just stand in front of him so he can smell you."

Kristen panicked when Colorado nuzzled her.

Mark laughed, "He won't hurt you. Kristen you look petrified. Okay, just stand still and I'll back him up a little. He smells your fear."

Kristen whispered, "I'm sorry Mark, I've never been this close to a horse before."

"I thought you said you had ridden?"

"No, that was me. I said I had ridden and I wasn't too old to try again."

"I'm sorry. Tomorrow I'll take you to see a smaller horse."

"No, that's okay. Maybe when I can go riding will be a better time for that."

"All right. I'll take him back to the barn and then I'll come back and we'll go to dinner at the big house."

"I haven't seen Pamela all day. Will she know when it's dinnertime?"

"She'll be riding in shortly with the ranch hands. We'll see her when we eat. I'm off to the barn."

Kristen followed him with her eyes. "He looks like the dreamy Marlboro man."

Suddenly, a group of horses rode by and one of the cowboys yelled, "Hi Mom."

Mrs Ross chuckled, "I think one of those cowboys was your daughter."

"Mark was right, this is a different way of life."

Finally, Mark came back to the house, went in and washed his hands then came out and sat beside Kristen.

"I'll go in and wash my hands and face and be right back."

"Take your time, Mrs Ross. We'll wait for you."

"A bunch of cowboys rode by a short time ago and one of them yelled, 'Hi Mom'. I think it was Pamela." Kristen reached out to hold Mark's hand. "I love it here."

"While I was in the barn I got a call..."

"Please don't tell me we have to head back to New York."

"No, no, nothing like that. Henry called. They're sure you'll decide to live here, so he and Alice want to buy a place out here and retire so they can be near Pamela *and* the new baby. They checked on the Internet for real estate in Anaconda. They think that would be close enough so Pamela could visit, but not so close that they'd get in our lives. Henry asked if we'd go tomorrow to look at the house they're interested in. I said we would. But then walking from the barn, I thought I should have asked you first."

"Sweetheart, I think that's a wonderful idea. Then Pamela won't be that far away from us when she visits with them."

"I've married an angel." He leaned over and kissed her.

Mrs Ross cleared her throat to let them know she was at the door.

"Let's head to my parents house for dinner and you can meet everyone. We might even get to see Pamela," he laughed. It was a short walk and Mark explained what each building was for, which barn held the horses and then pointed to another barn where the cows were.

Kristen asked which barn the cattle stayed in. And Mark did his best to keep a straight face. "The cattle stay out on the range and graze."

They could hear the laughing and talking before they reached the porch of the big house.

Mrs Ross asked what the brush things were at the door.

"That's so the cowboys can clean the bottoms of their boots before they go inside. You'll see those outside the post office, restaurants and stores in town."

They entered the huge kitchen. The greetings were tumultuous.

Kristen had never seen such a long table.

Mrs Ross sat at the first seat available. Mark and Kristen kept moving until they found two seats together at the other end of the table near Pamela.

"Excuse me, little lady, you're in my seat. Can I sit in your lap."

"Yes, just don't eat off my plate."

The cowboy and those around him burst out laughing. "Well, fellas, I think I've met my match. I'll just sit beside you. Do you belong to anybody?"

"Well, I'm here with Mark and his wife."

"Where's your husband?"

"He died twelve years ago."

"I'm sorry for your loss. Is that a New York accent I hear?"

"It is."

"I love it. Could you talk to me some more?"

Mrs Ross laughed, "I do believe you're flirting with me."

And a romance began that would last many, many years.

###

# Thank You

My deepest appreciation goes to:

Edward Karlewicz for his undying patience, expertise and editing abilities, even when I fought him tooth and nail.

Eric Bernard, Esq., for the detailed description of the American Bar Association/Criminal Defense Convention.

And my brother, Walter, my Armorer, for his knowledge of weapons.